I0659161

PLAYING FOR

her heart

A GAMERS NOVEL

MEGAN ERICKSON

Entangled Publishing, LLC
2614 South Timberline Road
Suite 109
Fort Collins, CO 80525
Visit our website at www.entangledpublishing.com.

Brazen is an imprint of Entangled Publishing, LLC. For more information on our titles, visit www.brazenbooks.com.

Edited by Heather Howland
Cover design by Heather Howland
Cover art from Shutterstock

Manufactured in the United States of America

First Edition August 2015

To every nerdy nerd who loves to cosplay: You keep doing you.

Chapter One

He was the perfect Breck.

There were other Breck cosplayers around the convention but on every one, something was off—whether it was the shade of blue of his shirt, or the way his sword was hung.

This guy, though…this guy's shirt was the perfect blue, that brilliant color that was so noticeable in the *Aric's Revenge* video game. It was a blue that was almost purple. Chloe had even looked it up, and she'd determined it was #2a23ff. Which she recognized was pretty damn dorky, but why cosplay if she didn't go all in?

This Breck had blond hair that was the exact length of the character. Was it his normal cut, or had he gotten it done for the convention? She wasn't sure which one she preferred. An actual, real-life Breck in the wild was like finding a four-leaf clover.

The man shifted where he stood leaning against a wall, and the muscles in his arms rippled beneath the thin linen cloth. He had a strong jaw and full lips. A sharp, straight nose. He was perfect in those tight tan breeches, his sword hanging at the perfect angle on his hip.

Chloe's hands self-consciously went to the corset of her Sari costume, and the satin fabric was slick under her fingertips. She stepped forward, her skirt swishing around her bare legs and brushing along her lace-up, knee-high boots. She'd sewn the ribbing into her gray corset and laced it herself. She'd agonized over the beige skirt, making sure the dirt patches matched up to Sari's in the game.

Cosplay was…well, it meant everything to her. It wasn't Halloween. She didn't cut holes out of a sheet and throw it over her head and declare herself a ghost. Oh no. This was Comic-Con. And this year's star attraction was *Aric's Revenge*, the wildly popular video game turned into a wildly popular movie that had made buckets of money.

She was dressed as Sari, an enslaved ex-princess who was held prisoner alongside Evelyn, the wife of the main character, Aric. In the game, Sari had fallen in love with Breck.

Which was exactly what she planned to do that night. Minus the love part.

Chloe wasn't the type of girl who met guys in a bar and made small talk about their lives and the weather and their jobs. No, she was the type of girl who dressed up and pretended to be someone else for one night of wild passion.

And then before he saw the real her, she left, back to her life in her lonely home office in her bare apartment. A life where she had a reclusive, damaged brother, and dead sister.

A life where she was destined to fail everyone.

She let herself feel the crowd around her, keeping an eye

on Breck. There was an energy in the air, one that was fueled by a sense of belonging, and Chloe fed off it as she always did, smiling when she heard the exclamations of thrilled kids and adults.

The Comic-Con, held in Philadelphia at a large hotel convention center, was well attended, the crowd a mix of cosplay and people in street clothes. Chloe had arrived the night before, checked into her hotel room, and finished up the last-minute fixes to her costume. All around her was excited chatter, the soundtrack of video games and movies blasting from the various booths.

She'd waited all year for this, especially because of the presence of the *Aric's Revenge* creators. In fact, she'd just listened to Austin Rivers give a beautiful speech about his involvement in the making of the game. It was her favorite of the year—the graphics were stellar, the storyline tight, the cast diverse.

And now she was here, as Sari, and had finally found her Breck.

As she drew closer to her target, he raised his head, and blue eyes as brilliant as his shirt pierced her. She had to check to be sure her false eyelashes were still on, that her corset hadn't unlaced, because those eyes…well, she swore for a minute that they saw through her disguise to the boring, freelance computer-debugging geek underneath.

She wasn't that girl. Not tonight. She needed a costume to approach gorgeous men like the one in front of her, whose blue eyes were now tracking down her body, all the way to her toes and back up.

But then her vision was no longer full of Breck, because a man had stepped in front of her, blocking her view.

She craned her neck and moved to go around the man, but then he sidestepped, right into her path. She glared at him. Or rather, she glared at...Doc Ock.

A Doc Ock who was leering at her.

For God's sake.

He twisted at the waist, so his metal octopus arms clanged together. Leaning into her, he pulled a string near his head so a claw snapped in her face. "Need a hand untying that corset, baby?" He held out his hands so that all four of his metal arms lifted. "Because I got six."

This was what was keeping her from Breck? A *Spider-Man* villain? She raised her eyebrows, emboldened by her costume so she could say what she never could without it. "Seriously? That's your come on?"

He blinked at her. "Uh, yeah I guess so."

"That's the best you could come up with?"

His lips twisted to the side. "Well, uh, how about, are you afraid of spiders? Because I can protect you."

She rolled her eyes. "Spiderman already beat you once and —"

And then her world tilted as someone gripped her waist and slung her over a hard shoulder. Then she was moving as the body who held her began walking. She protested with an *umph* and raised her head, watching Doc Ock stare after them with wide eyes, his metal arms clanking.

Chloe tried to get her wits together, remembering this was cosplay and she was Sari and how dare this guy pick her up? She turned her attention to her kidnapper. Or rather, his back. His blue-shirt-clad back. "Hey, put me down."

He did with a *thunk*, and once she righted her skirt and brushed her hair out of her face, she got a good look at

Breck. *Her* Breck.

Her incredibly hot rescuer.

She placed her hand on her hips and tried to keep the breathiness out of her voice, because *damn*. "I was doing just fine back there."

"I know you were," he said in a deep voice that skittered down her spine like fingers. "But I wasn't. Had enough of watching that guy trying to hit on you." Those full lips, so full they were almost feminine, twisted into a smile. "I wanted your attention. Because you're the best Sari I've seen today."

Chloe sucked in a breath. Oh yes, he'd do.

She smiled, grateful for her heavy makeup—black-lined eyes, rouged cheeks, and red, red lips. "You're an okay Breck, I guess."

He laughed, a short burst of sound that made her grin even wider.

"Okay? Only okay? Damn, woman, you're a tough audience. I hand-dyed this shirt, I'll have you know."

Never in her life did she think a man talking about dying his shirt would make her wet. But, oh God, she was a little turned on right now. "Ah, but did you slice your finger open on the plastic boning while sewing it into your corset?" She had a small bloodstain on the inner lining to prove it.

She'd never seen a man whose face was so expressive. He twisted it from humor to one of mock sympathy in an instant. "Oh my God! The horror! Did you see the healer, my dear Sari?"

He was so good, slipping back into character. Which worked for her, because he'd never learn her real name if she had any say over it. "A dab of ointment and a bandage and I'll live to see another day."

He held out his hand and she studied it. Not too calloused. Nails short and well maintained. He had a rather muscular frame, but she assumed that came from a gym. She took one step closer and placed her injured hand in his.

His fingers closed around hers briefly, his gaze on her face, then his eyes dropped to her hand. He studied it, twisting his wrist, until he found the injury on her forefinger. She'd placed an honest to God white bandage on it she'd made from an old bed sheet. A Band-Aid would have ruined her look.

His mouth quirked up at the corners as he took it in, and then he lifted his gaze, lowered his head, and pressed a kiss to her finger.

She held in a gasp as his lips brushed her skin, the warmth spreading through her limbs like wildfire.

The first time Breck touched Sari in the game, she'd just picked the lock of her cell with a dagger hidden in her skirt. With several other prisoners at her heels, she'd taken off at a dead sprint in the catacombs of the dungeon, only to run headlong into Breck, who was there with Aric. He'd hauled her over his shoulder and she'd fought him the whole way, pounding his huge muscled back while he ignored her like she was a fly.

He'd smacked her ass, told her if she didn't stop, he'd lock her away again.

And Sari, who was no dummy, stopped.

Chloe thought maybe she should be kicking and screaming. That maybe this Breck was a little too much for her to handle, with those laughing blue eyes and sensual lips. But she wanted to know what was under that blue shirt, what was behind the laces of his breeches. She wanted to know what else those fingers could do, the ones that were currently massaging her hand.

Plus, she had her armor. Sari would protect her. Sari would speak for her.

Sari could do what Chloe never could. Be who Chloe could never be.

His lips left her skin and then he tugged gently on her arm. Another step brought her against him, so the breast cups of her corset brushed against his chest.

"Do I have to haul you over my shoulder to have dinner with me, or will you come willingly?" he asked quietly.

So blue, his eyes. He was like a walking Ken doll. Chloe had only played Barbies because her sister had forced her to, and when Chloe did play, she always ended up with Ken and Barbie on the roof of the Dream House naked.

She wanted this Ken doll naked, too. But without that weird smooth plastic crotch.

"I'll come willingly," she responded.

He tilted his head and his eyes sparkled. "I might need to frisk you for daggers. I'm not sure those are allowed in the establishment I'm taking you to." His eyes sparkled.

She licked her lips, tempted to tell him to forget dinner, a bed was all that was needed. But instead, she nodded. "You can frisk me."

He raised an eyebrow as he slipped a hand beneath the waist high slit on her skirt. "What will I find, Sari?"

Those fingers started at her outer thigh and then traced inward, along the soft flesh on her inner thigh. She sucked in a breath. "What do you think?"

He paused when he touched the leather of her garter. A smile tipped his lips. "Ah, my Sari, never without a weapon."

She stepped back then, away from his touch and swirled her skirt around her legs. "No man will have his hand up my skirt. I think we're safe wherever you plan to take me."

He paused, then held his elbow out. "I like a woman who can defend herself."

She slipped her arm in his and they began to walk. "Well then, glad you found me."

. . .

She was the perfect Sari.

Grant Osprey hadn't actually planned to pick out a Sari to go with his Breck. He didn't really discriminate when it came to these things. He would have been fine with a Wonder Woman or Poison Ivy. That steampunk Queen of Hearts two years ago had been a full house in bed.

But this Sari…there was something about her. Plump red lips, huge cascading waves of chestnut-brown hair that brushed the top of her high ass. That was her real hair, he bet, not a wig. What he wouldn't give to wrap his fist in it while he took her from behind. She was a petite thing, and he imagined spanning her narrow waist with his other hand, watching the firm globes of her ass jolt with every stroke inside of her.

He was getting a little ahead of himself, but that's what these conventions were for him. Sure he dated here and there, but dating lead to complications that he simply didn't have time for. He was the owner of a gaming magazine and a stressed-out single dad. But here? He wasn't any of those things. He was Deadpool or Legolas or Breck.

He didn't have to fuck, but he sure as hell liked to, and

if Sari's glimmering green eyes were any indication, she did, too.

He glanced around the crowded convention for a glimpse of his friend, Austin Rivers, and his girlfriend, Marley Lake. But they'd just made up after a big fight so he was sure they were in a hotel right now fucking like bunnies.

Good for them. Marley was the newly appointed editor of *Gamers* and she was the only thing that made Austin happy. And it seemed the feeling was mutual.

Grant's eyes drifted to Sari's chest. The tops of her rounded breasts peeked out of the top of her corset. They looked soft and smooth and perfectly lickable. He had the urge to lay his head on them, run his fingers along the smooth satin fabric of her corset, listen to her heartbeat.

He led Sari to a small restaurant that had been set up near the *Aric's Revenge* stage. He glanced around but now that the presentation was over, the area was less crowded and he didn't see anyone he knew.

The inside of the restaurant had been made to look like a medieval tavern. Faux stone covered the walls, and the lighting was dim with electric sconces on the wall, which flickered to look like real firelight. A gas fireplace lit up the corner, a bearskin rug on the floor in front of it. There was an aisle down the center with large rectangular wooden tables on each side, about five deep, with benches for sitting.

The acoustics were terrible, but it settled Grant into the role, making him feel like he'd just completed his mission and was now dining with his spoils: Sari.

Grant ordered them some red wine and hot beef sandwiches. Sari sat with her legs crossed, the garter holding her dagger visible on one pale thigh. He wanted to drop to his knees under the table and shove his face between her legs, but he needed to have some modicum of decorum. This wasn't *actually* the Middle Ages.

Plus, he didn't know what she wanted. Flirting didn't mean she was going to get naked for him.

Her lashes were incredibly long, and he wondered if they were fake or real. His daughter, Sydney, had never been into makeup and was only getting started now that her high school friends were encouraging her. So Grant didn't know what to look for with these things. All he knew was that Sari was gorgeous. Stunningly so. Her shoulders were bare and slender. She wore an iron cuff on her biceps in the shape of a dragon. He had the sudden desire to see her calves, ankles, and feet hidden in her knee-high boots.

Grant had always been able to fall back on his charm. He flirted shamelessly with anyone with a pulse. But this woman tied up his tongue in knots. He took a sip of wine to lubricate it.

"Should I call you Sari or…"

She blinked slowly over the rim of her pewter cup. "Sari's fine."

Why did that make his dick hard? "Guess I'll remain Breck then."

The sandwiches were placed in front of them by a winking wench. Grant grinned back, and Sari laughed.

Grant poked at his sandwich, which oozed juice as it sat on a wooden trencher. They had cloth napkins but no silverware. He took a bite and savored the seasoned meat. "Tell me about where you're from."

He watched the tip of her tongue slip past those red lips and swipe at a bit of juice that had escaped out of the corner of her mouth. "Well, as you know, I'm a Princess."

Grant grinned, glad this was still the game. "I do, your Majesty."

"Your highness," she sniffed.

He stifled a snort at her offended frown. "Apologies."

She brushed her hair behind her shoulder. "Avaria is quite beautiful, you know, with…" Her voice faltered as she said, "butterflies and singing birds."

He dug his fingers into his thigh so he didn't burst into laughter. "You don't say. Butterflies and singing birds. Paradise, it sounds like."

"And meadows and lakes."

"Why, of course."

She licked her lips again, and they quirked at the corners, like she was trying to hold in a smile. "So when I was betrothed to an evil man in the neighboring kingdom, which was obviously dark and scary with no butterflies and singing birds…"

He nodded emphatically.

"I ran away. When I was finally captured, my betrothed had died. So my brothers sold me into slavery as punishment."

"Horrible and cruel."

"Indeed," she said, sipping her wine.

"But I saved you," he pointed out.

"Well, I had planned to save myself. You just beat me to it. Just like back with Doc Ock."

Feisty, this one. "Hmm."

She leaned closer, her chest almost brushing the top of her now-empty plate. "But, I-I guess I need to repay you, Breck. For saving me."

Now they were talking. He so wanted payment. "And

how do you plan to do so?"

"Well, I…" She looked uncertain, but it was an act, he could tell. "I don't have any money. No land or titles anymore. But…" She leaned even closer and he met her halfway, so close he could feel her hot breath on his lips. Those lashes might have brushed his own cheeks if he was any closer. "I have my body, Breck. I can repay you with that."

He was so fucking hard in his goddamn tight breeches that it was painful. He wanted to unlace them, pull out his cock, and take her body right then, right there.

Her eyes were glittering emeralds; her lips parted.

"You think that hot little body of yours is enough to repay me, Princess?" he whispered.

Her pupils dilated and she squirmed a little in her seat. "I'm well educated on how to please a man."

He wanted that corset off. He wanted that skirt pooled at her feet. He wanted those breasts in his hands and his cock slipping between her wet folds. But first he needed to make sure they were on the same page. "Is this a one-time deal, then?"

She didn't hesitate. "Yes."

Game. Fucking. On. "Then let's retreat to my bedchamber."

He tossed a handful of bills on the table, hauled her to her feet, and strode in the direction of his hotel room with a single-minded focus. He was going to take his Sari.

Chapter Two

The door to the hotel room snicked closed behind Chloe and she leaned back against it, getting her bearings by placing her palms flat on the door. She'd done this before, but it had been a while. She craved a man's touch and it had been so long since she'd had sex, she wondered if she'd remember how it all worked. Thank God Breck had come along so she didn't have to break her spell with a guy who had four metal arms. And creepy metal clamps.

Breck stood with his back to her, unbuckling the sword from around his waist and placing it on the dresser beside the TV.

Chloe closed her eyes. She was someone else here in this hotel room. This man didn't know her name, and she didn't know his. She could let herself go, get her pleasure, and then leave.

It was what he wanted, too, based on their agreement at the restaurant.

She opened her eyes, took a deep breath, and walked toward him. He turned around, his hands at the loosened laces at the top of his shirt. She watched as he took it off by grasping the fabric with one hand between his shoulder blades and tugging it off. He dropped it to the side, and it fluttered to the floor.

He was mostly hairless, and had a gorgeously muscled chest. She itched to reach out and run a caressing hand over his collarbone and shoulders. A line of fine blond hair began below his belly button and led down to his waistband. Her gaze descended farther, until it landed on the bulge in his pants.

"Do I get to enjoy my payment now?" he asked, a smirk on his lips, but breathlessness he couldn't hide belying his excitement.

She turned around, presenting her back to him, and then looked at him over her shoulder from under her lashes. "You'll have to untie my corset."

She faced forward and waited. Several seconds later the heat of his chest coated her back and she waited for the tugging on the corset to begin. But instead he took her hair and pulled it to the side, dropping it over her shoulder so it fell down her chest. She'd always worn her hair long, but for this event, she'd let it go until it touched the top of her ass. Monday, she had an appointment to cut it all off. She enjoyed the feel of the weight while she still could, the slight tugging as Breck touched a lock of it. Then his fingers brushed the back of her neck, just a slight touch, and his lips closed around her earlobe. He sucked the delicate skin into his mouth, nibbling slightly, and she gasped.

He released her earlobe and left a blazing trail of

lips, tongue, and teeth down her neck and along her bare
shoulder. She turned her head, and raised her hand, slipping
it into his thick blond hair.

He lifted his head, blue eyes blazing. They were as
intense if not more so without the blue shirt on. "It's been a
long time since I had a woman, Sari," he rasped. "Not sure I
can be gentle with you."

She swallowed, speaking for Chloe *and* Sari. "I like it
rough."

The tug on the corset strings was sharp, and she grunted
a little as her body slammed into his. He still watched her,
those blue eyes on her face as his fingers tugged at the laces.
She wasn't sure how he was doing it without looking, but she
didn't care, because she couldn't look away from his gaze,
the way those blue orbs caressed her face.

He didn't just loosen the corset; he slipped all the laces
through the rivets she'd hand stamped until the corset fell
from her body onto the floor. Her nipples, sensitive from her
arousal, tightened in the cool air of the hotel room, and she
sucked in a breath.

Her first instinct was to cover them and run into the
bathroom. This was always the part that threw her. She had
to get naked. She had to take off the costume that was her
armor.

But then she slipped back into her role. It wasn't just the
clothes. It was the attitude, the anonymity of the fake name.
It was the realization that this man could be from anywhere,
having only flown in to attend the con. And that's what kept
her hands at her sides as his fingers dug into the skin at her
waist. His breath rushed along her temple as he stared down
at her bared breasts.

His fingers grazed her ribs as he lifted his hands and then cupped her. "These are gorgeous, Princess. I'm going to take you from behind, and then I'll have to rally for another round because I want to suck on these while I'm inside you."

She reached around and grasped his thigh, digging her nails into the thin fabric to tell him yes, yes she loved the sound of that, even though she wasn't sure she could articulate it in words right now.

A guy talking dirty made her hot. If porn was nothing but grunts, she turned it off. She wanted dirty talk. Filthy. Breck was delivering already, and they were only topless.

"You want that, Princess?" He pinched her nipples, rolling them between his thumbs and forefingers before letting them go. He gave each of them a sharp slap on the underside, the sound echoing off the walls. She moaned, and wondered if he could make her come just by playing with her breasts.

She wouldn't have minded the experiment.

He splayed one hand across her waist and tucked her tighter against him, so she felt his erection at the small of her back. Then with his other hand, he gripped the edge of her skirt where it was slit and pulled it aside. She wore a pair of flesh-colored panties underneath, which he promptly shoved down her legs and ordered her to step out of. Then she was upright again, smashed against his chest. And he was swiping two fingers through her folds.

"You *do* want that," he said, his voice lower with arousal. "Fuck. So wet, Princess." Those fingers didn't stop, swirling and rubbing and doing all kinds of crazy things. He found her clit but did nothing but give it a cursory pinch, which made her growl. He chuckled darkly.

In a swift motion, he stepped away from her and then

she was pushed onto the bed on her back. Her legs dangled over the edge, her skirt in disarray around her. She leaned up on her elbows as he stood at the foot of the bed in front of her. His eyes roamed her face, breasts and then lingered on her thighs. "So beautiful. Spread your legs."

She did so slowly, propping the heel of one boot on the comforter, then the other, so she was bared to him.

He reached down and palmed the bulge in his pants, stroking himself through the fabric. It was obscene how hard he was and how thin those pants were. She could see the flared head of his cock, the outline of his shaft and she bit her lip, imagining it in her mouth.

His hand moved away and her gaze snapped up to his face. "Oh, you'll get my cock, Princess. But not yet."

With a *thud*, he fell to his knees, grinned at her, and lowered his head between her legs.

At first she felt nothing, only the heat of his breath on her wet, sensitive flesh. Then his hands slowly gripped her thighs. She was tugged so her ass almost hung off the bed and then…just when she was about to reach down and push his face into her sensitive flesh, he licked.

One. Long. Slow. Lick. Until he reached her clit, and then he swirled the tip around the hard bud.

He did it again. That long, slow torturous lick with the swirl on the end. He varied the pace a little. Sometimes the lick was faster. Sometimes it was so slow, she didn't think he'd ever get to that fancy swirl at the end.

She squirmed and balled the comforter in her fists and gasped out her breath in pants. Just when she thought she couldn't take enough, he stopped.

And then the tongue-fucking began.

No one had ever done that to her, but this man, God what a tongue he had on him. He must've practiced on something, because it was exquisite the way he worked her entrance.

By the time he moved back to her clit, she was a stuttering mess. She didn't know who she was supposed to be anymore. Hell, she didn't even know her real name, if he asked. All she knew was this man was leaving bruises where he clutched her thighs and his tongue was making her come and she never wanted this moment to end.

Her climax was a force, curling her toes in her boots, clawing her fingers, and arching her back as she sobbed out a cracked scream. For a second she swore her heart stopped with the force of the reaction that shocked her body.

When she came to, limp on the bed, Breck's head was on her thigh, his hands stroking her belly.

She brushed her hair off her forehead and tried for a smile, although she knew it was thin. Chloe didn't think all the muscles in her face worked yet. "How'd a soldier like you learn how to lick a woman like that?"

He laughed, his lips swollen and wet from his attention to her. "I can't share all my secrets."

He rose slowly to his feet, unlaced his pants, and dropped trough.

His cock stood out from a thatch of blond hair. She managed to gather her elbows under herself and rise slightly to get a better look.

His thighs were muscular, covered with soft golden hair and she wanted to sit up, stroke her hands up the back of those legs, grab his ass, and suck on his rigid length.

As if he knew what she was thinking, his lips quirked and he wrapped his hand around his shaft and stroked slowly.

Once. Twice. The third time he added a twist at the tip and the head glistened with moisture. She licked her lips, and he took a step forward.

"Can you sit up, Princess?"

She huffed a little under her breath. "You think me weak?"

His laugh was short. "You're anything but."

She sat up, and his hand rested on the back of her head, guiding it toward where he grasped his shaft in a tight fist. Instead of asking her to open her mouth, he painted her lips with his slick tip. He smelled like a mix of sex, cologne, and wine. It was heady and for a while, as he teased the head of his cock between her lips and back out again, she forgot where she was. She only existed here, in this moment, to give this man pleasure and receive it in return. She closed her eyes, savoring the flavor, the weight of a cock on her tongue.

And then she hollowed out her cheeks and began to bob her head.

"Fuck," Breck swore under his breath. His cock left her mouth abruptly and when she opened her eyes, his cock was angry and red, and he was holding the base tightly.

A muscle in his jaw clenched. "First time I come inside you, it's sure as fuck not going to be your mouth."

His words shot a bolt of lust down her spine and her inner muscles clenched.

He bent down, grabbed something from his pants, and then she was flat on her back, a naked man on top of her, his hips snugged between her thighs…

And he was kissing her.

His lips were so hot she swore he was burning the skin off hers. His tongue was swirling, dueling with hers in an imitation of what he'd done between her legs.

When he broke off the kiss and began working his way across her jaw and down her neck, that's when she realized this was the first time he'd kissed her. They hadn't done it when she walked into the hotel room. He'd licked her to orgasm, and she'd sucked him like a lollipop, all before they ever got their tongues in each other's mouths.

It felt kind of *Pretty Woman*-ish.

Chloe wrapped her legs around Breck's naked hips, her skirt open on the bed around them. She imagined she looked thoroughly debauched—bare-breasted, skirt thrown up around her hips while he fucked her.

He was thrusting against her, his bare cock, hard as steel, slipping between her wet folds. She could hear it, the obscene sounds of it, and she would have been embarrassed at how wet she was, of the mess she was making, if she was anyone but Sari.

It seemed to spur Breck on. He reached down between them and rubbed his cock over her clit. "You're so fucking wet, Princess," he gasped, then licked a nipple and bit it gently. "Love how wet you are."

He lifted his gaze, locked eyes with her, then stuck out his tongue, flicking her nipple once, twice, before moving on to the other one. God, that tongue. What more could he do with that thing? She wondered if he practiced knotting cherry stems. Or maybe he'd worked up to something stronger and could bend paperclips with it. That'd be something.

He smiled then, a wicked one that made him look like a teenager about to drink for the first time. Then his mouth was on hers again, and she heard the crinkle of a condom wrapper.

He pulled back and sat on his heels between her legs. He took her right foot and slowly began to undo the laces to her boots. She squirmed, but let him work, watching as he pulled off her boot and placed a kiss on the inside of her ankle bone, his lips slipping up her calf. Then he proceeded to do the same to her other foot, his fingers lingering on her high arch, his lips circling her anklebone. He dropped her legs back onto the bed, and reached for the condom. Once he rolled it down his length, he eyed her, gaze roaming her face, lingering on her breasts, then down her belly and between her legs. The slit in her skirt was so high that it was really only belted around her waist now, the fabric open like flaps on either side of her legs.

His hands started at her collarbone, trailing fingertips down her skin, leaving goose bumps in their wake. When he reached her hips, his eyes flashed, before she was quickly turned onto her stomach. She squealed at the change, and he hauled her up onto her knees. She gathered her hands under her, eyes on the olive-green sheet as he tugged up her skirt to her waist, so her ass was exposed.

The slap was swift, stinging, and fucking hot. The pain bloomed over her right cheek before his palm rubbed the sting away. Then he smacked the left cheek and she moaned as more moisture surged between her legs.

She was Sari. Ex-Princess. Using her body as payment to her soldier rescuer. And she wasn't sure she'd ever been so eager for this in her life.

"Ready for my cock, Princess?" Breck's voice was low, tight, like he was hanging on by a thread.

She sucked in a breath and wiggled her ass. "Fuck me, Soldier."

He gripped her hips and sheathed himself inside of her to the hilt.

She screamed and fell to her elbows, surprised at his strength and size. A hand coasted over the top of her ass. She flexed and arched her spine, urging him to move, and with bruising fingers gripping the cheeks of her ass, he did.

"Harder," she urged. "Fuck me, harder."

He responded with a punishing rhythm. Each thrust of his hips hit something inside of her she wasn't sure she ever felt before. She was aware of a feeling in her lower belly, a wet heat, and every time his cock plunged inside, she saw stars. The walls echoed with the sounds of slapping skin.

"You're so wet," he gasped out, gripping her ass tighter. "Fuck yourself on my dick, sweetheart." She reared back, half mad with lust now, searching for whatever was causing her bones to liquefy. They found their rhythm and the sound of her breath was like a roaring in her ears.

Fingers touched her clit and she wasn't sure if they were hers, or if they were his. All she knew was they were working in tandem with that spot inside her body. Whatever this thing was felt big and terrifying and part of her wanted to call this all off, just get off this bed and run to the bathroom, because this, this felt like a tsunami that would sweep her out to sea.

"Come on, Princess." Breck's voice was a rasp. "I can feel that pussy squeezing me. Come on my cock."

She would. She could feel it building. "Breck," she sobbed out.

"Fuck," he gasped out.

His right hand left her hip and then a crack rent the air where he smacked her flesh. And that was all she needed, that extra heat, because now she was coming, crying out in a wrecked voice, heaving unintelligible words as Breck growled behind her, his hips stuttering, his cock pulsing inside of her as she milked him.

Her arms gave out from under her and she collapsed onto the bed, at least remembering to turn her head so she didn't smash her nose. She needed to breathe. She needed to be sure she still had all her limbs.

The bed thumped near her head, and a balled fist appeared, clutching the sheets. Hair brushed along the top of her back between her shoulder blades, then a weight there, like he was resting his forehead. As she closed her eyes, she became aware of his breath, hot on the clammy skin of her back.

He was still inside her; she could feel him there, softening slightly. With a groan, he pulled out slowly and she didn't even bother closing her legs like she normally would have. She remained on her stomach, exhausted, as she heard him pad to the bathroom and flush the toilet. When he returned, the bed dipped beside her. Fingers drifted down her spine. He rubbed her skin where he'd smacked her, and she squirmed a little. It stung now, the skin tight and hot.

The hand left, and then something else was there, something wet, and she realized he was kissing the flesh he'd abused.

Chloe opened her eyes and stared sightlessly at the beige wall. His lips were wonderful on her skin, and he was adding tongue now, leaving a trail of wetness behind.

Finally, his face came into view, and he pressed a kiss to her temple. "Ah, Princess. You sure know how to pay a debt."

She raised her fist to her mouth and bit it as she giggled. His responding laughter only made her giggle harder, until he collapsed on the bed beside her, clutching his stomach, his blue eyes sparkling.

Her anticipation of sex often gave her rose glasses with men. She expected Breck to look like a poor man's version of the one she'd originally walked into this hotel with. But if possible he was even better-looking. His lips were swollen, cheeks rosy. His hair was a mess but his eyes…they were still full of humor. And he was still looking at her like she was the princess of his dreams.

Which sobered her a little. She was no princess. Without this persona to hide behind, she wasn't anything worth keeping.

His smile dimmed and he raised a hand, brushing the backs of his fingers down her cheek. "That good for you, Princess?"

"Once you go Breck, you never go back."

He barked out a laugh, his eyes twinkling again. "You're my walking, talking fantasy, you know that?"

Sari was his fantasy. "You're pretty dreamy yourself."

He picked up a lock of her hair and fingered it, winding it around his forefinger and running his thumb over the strands. "Such beautiful hair."

She had to swallow through the thickness in her throat. Her hair might be way longer than normal, but that was all her. That was Chloe's hair. "Thank you."

His gaze lifted to her and he hesitated before saying softly, "Want to rest a little, then maybe…see what other positions we can come up with?"

She moved her weary limbs until her skirt was in a pool

at the foot of the bed. Breck took that as a sign and pulled the covers out from under them and covered their bodies.

"Yeah," she said with a yawn. "Let's do that."

Breck smiled and pulled her close, tucking her head under his chin.

He took a deep breath, and it wasn't even five minutes later when his hold on her relaxed and his breaths evened out.

She lay awake for another hour after that, enjoying his strong arms around her, the beat of his heart, the heat of his skin, the smell of man.

Who knew when she'd get this again, and she was smart enough to know the sex they'd had was a once-in-a-lifetime experience.

She didn't even know his real name.

But it was better this way. She'd forever be a fantasy to him. She'd remain on a pedestal where she'd always be perfect. He'd never have to listen to her cry over the family she'd been unable to prevent from fracturing. He'd never have to hear her worry about her how her brother was handling his guilt. He'd never have to know that she, Chloe Talley, was about as interesting as a doorknob, and that she should have been the sister who passed away in that car accident years ago, not Samantha, the glue who held everyone together.

Nope, he'd always remember her as Sari, the princess who fucked like a queen.

And that was why she carefully slipped out of his arms as he slept, dressed quietly in the dark, and tiptoed out of the hotel room, shutting the door softly behind her.

Chapter Three

If anyone knew that Grant listened to Pink and Christina Aguilera while exercising instead of Metallica or something suitably masculine, he'd never live it down.

But hot damn, he loved this song. Xtina sang "Fighter" and he tossed his head along with the song, now adept at shimmying on the treadmill at the same time his feet pounded the tread. He was alone in his basement, so he could act the fool all he wanted.

He ran shirtless and the sweat dripped down his back, soaking the waistband of his mesh shorts. He upped the incline with a couple jabs of his index finger and ran harder, pushing himself to the brink, needing to reach that point of exhaustion.

Ever since he woke up a week ago in that hotel room, naked and alone, he'd tried to convince himself that he'd dodged a bullet. That she'd spared him the awkward morning after where they both tried to cover up their private parts while guzzling coffee.

Except…nothing about his time with Sari had been awkward. Not at all. She'd been so responsive to his touch. She'd loved everything he did, every word, every flick of his tongue. Her eyes were heated missiles and he still felt the burns.

So while he'd tried to tell himself it was for the best, when he was alone in the shower, his hand circling his stiff cock, he lamented missing out on round two.

And when he was lying awake in bed at night—because insomnia had decided to become his friend lately—he realized that he also he cared that he didn't say good-bye. That he didn't get her real name.

Maybe it was the way she talked, or the way she moved. The way she threw herself into the role, the way she clearly knew the video game inside and out. Either way, the sum of Sari had made him want to break all his rules, because that woman was worth it.

But she'd stolen out of the room while he'd been passed out in a post-orgasmic deep sleep. He'd almost thought he dreamed it, until he found her panties under the bed skirt.

Grant had brought them home, like some lovesick idiot, tucked into his bag. If Sydney ever found them… Hell he'd probably lie and said he cross-dressed rather than admit to bringing home a stranger's underwear. Because didn't that make him a super creep?

He couldn't stop thinking about her, the way her large breasts felt in his hands, the way she tasted, the way her sweet pussy clenched around his cock as she came apart below him, her cries echoing in his ears. His palms itched sometimes, a phantom sting where he'd cracked them on the flesh of her ass.

He'd searched the convention for her, but it had been Sunday, the last day. He knew his chances of finding her again were slim, but he'd been desperate.

Grant didn't do desperate.

So maybe it was better this way. He could remember Sari as she was, a beautiful vixen, and move on with his life. He was a single father with a teenage daughter. Complications and attachments weren't his thing. But even as Sydney's shadow fell across the floor in front of his treadmill, he had a hard time remembering that.

He popped his earbuds out of his ears, causing Pink's voice to fade away, as he lowered the incline of the treadmill and slowed the speed. "What's up?"

His daughter propped an elbow on the front console. "Taste-testing time."

This was why he worked out. Because if he didn't, his daughter would surely turn him into a five-hundred-pound man. She loved to bake, and he'd told her he'd send her to culinary school if that was what she wanted. She insisted, though, that this was her hobby. One she loved and planned to keep but it was exactly that, a hobby. It was a good one, too. Sydney had a peanut allergy and baked goods were some of the hardest to find allergy-free.

Sydney wanted to follow in her father's footsteps and enter the tech world as a programmer. He was proud of her, because after cooking, she was always at her computer. More women were needed in STEM occupations. Hell, at *Gamers*, the magazine he owned, Marley was only one of three women out of fifty employees. It wasn't that Grant didn't want to hire them, it was that he didn't have many applicants.

He sniffed the air. She'd left the basement door open and the sweet smell had begun to drift down the stairs. He walked slowly, wiping down his face and upper body with a towel he hooked onto the arm bar. "What'd you make?"

"Lavender shortbread cookies with a lemon glaze."

"Damn." He reached for his bottle in the treadmill's cup holder and squirted water in his mouth. "Sounds amazing."

Sydney was blond, like him, with big blue eyes. She had her mother's face, the small mouth and nose, deep-set eyes. Her hair was pulled up into a ponytail, and she wore her red gingham apron, which was pretty much her Saturday look, since she spent most of it in the kitchen. He encouraged her to spend time with friends but she was diligent, his girl. A hard worker. Like father, like daughter.

Her brows drew together when she frowned. "I'm not sure if the glaze is the right consistency. And I made the cookies two different thicknesses, a quarter inch and half inch."

She always did this, talked at him but didn't really expect him to answer. Which was a good thing because he knew next to nothing about baking. He could make a mean burrito, though.

"I want you to tell me which you think baked up the best. And if you like the glaze." She was already walking away and called over her shoulder. "But take a shower first, because you stink."

He shook his head. Sydney was such an old soul, practically mothering him. Since she'd grown up with an incredibly distant mother, Sydney assumed the role for herself. Grant was only one person and maybe too much of a kid at heart.

After all, he still dressed up and got laid in costume. If

that didn't say sixteen-year-old nerd, he didn't know what did.

He walked past the sweet-smelling kitchen where Sydney puttered around and headed right to his bathroom, dropping his shorts and toeing off his shoes before stepping into the shower and turning on the spray.

His legs felt a little like jelly, but the hot water soothed his muscles.

Grant had been a freshman in college when a girl he'd slept with came to him with a tear-streaked face and a positive pregnancy test. She wanted to give the baby up for adoption, but Grant had said that he'd take her. His parents helped and even at the toughest of times, he didn't regret his decision. Sydney's mother, Avery, saw her a couple of times a year, but Avery now had a new husband on the opposite coast of the US. Her relationship with Sydney was strained and neither seemed to have the urge to change it.

He stepped out of the shower and wrapped a towel around his waist. The smell of the cookies was strong now, and Grant smiled. Life was good. Maybe in time, he could forget about the princess. Time healed everything right?

In his bedroom, he pulled on a pair of old sweats, and trotted out to get his treats.

• • •

Chloe stirred the sausage tortilla soup in her brand-new blue Le Creuset pot. Even at seventy percent off, the pot had been a total splurge, but she figured she deserved it. Her small apartment was furnished, and the only real money she spent on clothes was for cosplay. So since she'd just finished up a big job, she'd bought what she really wanted.

Cooking was like therapy for her. The act of taking unrelated ingredients and molding them, mixing them into something delicious, was like a balm to her soul. There was no pressure. No one or nothing to let down. She cooked for herself so if she screwed something up, no one knew but her.

She didn't have to talk to anyone. Well, she did talk to her ingredients. And her dishes. She'd already told her pot that she loved it. But they didn't talk back, which was the best part about them.

The sausage tortilla soup was a new recipe she'd seen on Pinterest. Her profile on that site was an odd amalgamation of recipes, video-game cheats, and cosplay costume ideas. That fit her and her mind, which was a complete hodgepodge of information.

She stirred the soup one last time and then propped her spoon on her cat-shaped spoon rest. It had been a housewarming present from her brother Ethan. She was touched, because her cat had died shortly before her move. She'd planned to get a new pet but she needed time to mourn Chester.

She smiled, thinking of Ethan picking out a spoon rest for her. She couldn't imagine he bought it in person, but even the thought of her brother googling something like that made her giggle.

There had been an Ethan years ago that would have easily charmed his way into some kitschy boutique to look for a present for her.

But that was before the accident. Before he'd taken their sister for a ride in his fancy new sports car. Before he took a turn going too fast, showing off. Before the tires slid on gravel and the whole car flipped.

Before Samantha Talley died of a broken neck and Ethan landed in the hospital recovering from third-degree burns, leaving him covered in scars.

That had been over two years ago and Ethan spent every single day since then beating himself up with guilt. Chloe understood the guilt, but it was an accident. She wished Ethan could see that. She loved her brother, always would. She knew he'd never be the Ethan he was before, but this one was hard to bear sometimes, the guilt often visible in every line of his face.

Her cell rang from its spot on the counter. She glanced at the screen and thought about ignoring it, but she knew her mother would just call again. Chloe worked from home, so she didn't have much of an excuse, even if it was a Saturday.

She picked it up and answered, settling it into the crook of her shoulder while she began to clean up from preparing the soup. "Hello?"

"Hey, Chloe, it's Mom."

She pictured her mom sitting at the kitchen table, staring out her large bay windows at the backyard, where she had just about every bird feeder known to man. "Hey, Mom."

"Did you do anything last weekend?"

Well, last weekend, she'd been dressed as a warrior princess, getting screwed in a hotel room by a stranger. Her face flamed. "No, not much, just worked."

"And are you settling into your apartment okay?"

She glanced around. It was small, but she didn't need anything big. The complex itself was fairly new. The walls were painted a nice cream and the wood floors were a warm honey color. She'd found a blue braided rug on sale, which went well with her blue-and-tan checked couch. Admittedly the couch pattern was a little ugly but it was the most comfortable damn couch she'd ever sat on. "Yeah, Mom, I really like it."

"You know, you could have moved closer to us instead…" Her voice trailed off.

Chloe dug her nails into her palms until the pain focused her. This was the problem, and had been the problem since Samantha died. Her parents refused to admit they blamed Ethan for Samantha's death, but it was evident in the way they treated him. Ethan *did* blame himself, and exiling himself from their parents was this self-imposed punishment. He'd been the driver; he was the one who'd lost control of the car.

He'd told Chloe he didn't want to repair the relationship. Ethan didn't want to see the consequences of his actions any more than her parents wanted to forgive one of their children for the death of another. No one was at fault and yet everyone was at fault.

Or really, it was just one stupid accident.

Either way, Chloe was caught in the middle of a tug of war that was never-ending. Samantha had been the effervescent daughter who held the Talley family together. She'd been the one to smooth everything over with charm and class. With her gone, there was no glue and the Talley family members were all loose orbits, spinning off into space. No matter how hard Chloe tried, she couldn't bring them together, couldn't ground them. She'd never been able to.

And after her sister's death, it had never been more apparent that Chloe *was* never and *could* never be Samantha.

Chloe wanted to fill that hole for her family, but it was

becoming rapidly apparent no one could, because that hole had grown larger than life. Her sister had always been the prettier one, the outspoken one. And now that Samantha was gone, she was frozen in time as the beautiful, charming, utterly *perfect* woman.

Chloe struggled in this weird new role as the remaining Talley daughter. She'd known who she was before, quiet sister to her gregarious older siblings. She'd been the baby, content to remain in the shadows, proud of her beautiful sister and successful brother.

Until the accident, which turned Ethan into the black sheep while her parents suddenly remembered Chloe existed. Their attention had been stifling, consuming, as they seemed to want to wrap her in a protective bubble. Chloe didn't know how to react under this microscope, what to do, and everything she *did* do seemed to make it worse.

She filled a glass of water and took a couple of gulps. "I know, Mom, but Ethan asked me to move closer and I… I like it here."

"I see." Her voice was tight.

"Ethan is…" *Good* wasn't really accurate, but she felt the need to talk about him, remind her mother she had a son. "Busy. He recently bought half of a magazine company."

Her mother didn't respond. It was like Ethan didn't exist. The tension leaked through the phone like poisoned gas.

"D-do you want me to have him call you?"

Her voice came quickly. "I don't want Ethan to feel forced to speak to his parents."

Chloe bit her lip. "Um, yeah, okay. I get that." Why couldn't she find the right words to say, the sandpaper to smooth away the rough edges in her mom's voice? Samantha could have done that in her sleep. "You could visit me, if you want."

"I'll speak to your father." She sounded distracted now. "I just wanted to call and check on my daughter. Do you have plans today?"

"I'm trying a new recipe."

"And plans to be social? I looked up some places that have singles nights."

Singles nights. Good God, those words were like a shot of pure terror right into her blood. This was the problem. As the only remaining child her parents spoke to, she was smothered by their well-intentioned advice. "Uh-uh, no, Mom. That's all right. Maybe I'll call Ethan and —"

"I'm sure he has some single friends that are upstanding in the community."

Chloe could barely converse in public, the least of her concerns was her hypothetical date's social status. "Sure."

"Great, speak to him about that."

"Okay."

"I'll tell your father you said hello. Have a nice day, sweetie."

"Bye, Mom."

Chloe hung up the phone and tossed it onto the counter with a clatter. She'd made it through that conversation in one piece, and yet, she wanted to crawl under her covers. Or throw herself into work. Other than anonymous sex, being an introvert and working her ass off were the only skills she excelled at.

But the older she got, the more she wondered if there was more to life. There had been for her at one time, before everything crumbled around her.

Instead of retreating to a bedsheets cave, she took a bath, in the middle of a Saturday morning, like the grownup she was, using a bath bomb that made her whole bathroom smell like lavender. She loved her claw-footed tub, which she'd brought from her last apartment and had installed immediately.

She wrapped her e-reader in two plastic storage bags and read a romance novel full of sweet kissing and heavy petting.

In the past, that would have been enough to get her hot, to maybe touch herself with pruney fingers beneath the water. But now, her eyes glossed over the words, wanting to read something dirtier with a hero who talked like Breck, who handled a woman's body as deftly as he'd handled hers.

She dropped her kindle on the mat and closed her eyes, leaning back in the tub as she imagined Breck was sitting in the opposite side of the tub. First, he'd tell her to bend over and clutch the edge of the tub, so her ass was facing him. He'd smack it, play with her, running his fingers over her slick flesh until she was begging.

Chloe ran her hand down her belly and stroked her folds under the water, feeling the slickness that was her own making. She swirled the pad of her middle finger over her clit, imagined it was Breck's hand.

He'd tell her to straddle his waist, and she would, impaling herself on his cock as he sucked on her nipples and palmed her breasts. She'd ride him, hard. And she'd change the angle until she found that spot that he'd awakened that night in the hotel room. The spot inside that had made her see stars.

Chloe opened her mouth, groaning, feeling the orgasm

start in her curled toes. Breck was urging her on now, pulling her hair, gripping her ass tightly under the water as she cried out. He'd bite the tender skin at her shoulder as he came inside of her.

When Chloe opened her eyes, there was water sloshed out on the floor all around the tub, and the remaining water had cooled.

She laughed to herself, thinking that while that had been a poor substitute for the man, it'd been the best self-love session she'd ever had. "Thanks for that, Breck," she muttered as she stepped out of the tub and grabbed a towel.

In her bedroom, she was dressing in a pair of loose gaucho pants and a large T-shirt, because she sure as heck wasn't going out in public, when the doorbell rang.

With a towel wrapped around her head, she made her way to the front door and peered through the peephole. As suspected, her brother stood at the door, holding a white paper bag, staring expectantly at the doorknob.

She thunked her head on the door, making a note to buy a secret cabin somewhere no one could find her, and then opened it. Ethan brushed past her, eyes scanning the apartment. He sniffed the air as he placed the paper bag on her kitchen counter. "What smells so good?"

"Sausage tortellini soup." He made an eager face and she rolled her eyes. "Yes, you can have some."

Ethan smiled, and Chloe thought that she'd make that soup every day of Ethan's life if she got a smile like that out of him. He didn't do it nearly as often anymore, which sucked because he used to be the fun one of the three of them, the carefree daredevil. He teased Chloe, and joked with her and Samantha about boys.

And then the accident happened, Samantha died, and it was like Ethan had a personality transplant. And because she loved him, she let him fret over her like a mother hen, knowing he felt like he had a debt to repay. Taking care of the sister who was still alive was the way he coped, and although it was unhealthy, it was the only mechanism he had. He'd refused to go to counseling, and she couldn't fix him, even through she'd tried. So she avoided any topics that would make him anxious, did everything she could to keep him happy, and let him fuss and dote, as long as it made him feel better.

Which was exhausting, to be honest.

He gestured to the bag. "I brought you some of those chocolate chip sugar cakes you like."

That got her feet moving. In a flash she was at the counter, peering into the bag. "Really? You didn't have to do that." She took out a sugar cake and bit into it immediately. It was perfect, absolutely perfect. Sugar cakes were like a large cookie but softer, more like a dense cake. And the top layer had the perfect sprinkle of sugar that had melted and cracked in the oven so there was just the slightest bit of crispness. She moaned. "You're my favorite brother ever."

His smile didn't fade, and she beamed at him. He was a handsome man, beyond handsome. Every single one of Chloe's and Samantha's friends had crushed on star baseball pitcher Ethan Talley.

Despite the visible scars, he was just as handsome in Chloe's mind, even if he didn't think so.

"I'm having dinner with my new business partner, Grant. He was a friend of mine in college."

She vaguely remembered the name. "Okay."

"I'd like you to come."

The sugar cake didn't taste so good anymore. She moved to the fridge to pour herself a glass of milk, buying time. She hated saying no to Ethan. "Why do you want me to come?" She'd never gone on any business dinners before. Ethan had his hands in a lot of pies, always had. He'd gotten rich quick in college by commentating while playing video games and uploading the videos to YouTube. He had the personality and the skill to cultivate a huge following, which turned into a huge source of income from advertising revenue. Turned out, that money was more of a curse than a blessing, at least in Chloe's mind. She wasn't sure how Ethan felt. He'd only seemed to have gotten richer since then, although he wasn't reckless anymore, and didn't flaunt it. His car and his house were his only visible splurges.

Okay, he had some great clothes, too. And that watch looked new.

"I think it'd be good to get you out of the house."

She rolled her eyes. "Ethan, you don't have to spend so much effort getting me to be social. I don't need a keeper."

He frowned. "Well, I'd also like to include you in what I do. In my life," he said.

She drank down her milk and studied Ethan. He seemed slightly uncomfortable, admitting that he wanted his little sister involved in his life. And even though attending one of his business dinners sounded like torture, she was touched he wanted her involved in his life. "When is it?"

"Thursday."

"Dress code."

He hesitated. "It's a nice place. Men wear jackets."

Great, so no gaucho pants. Thank God for online

shopping. "Okay."

There was that smile again. "Great, I'll text you place and time."

"Is that why you bought me sugar cakes? To butter me up?"

He smirked. "Nah, just thought you were getting too skinny. So, when's the soup going to be ready?"

Chloe turned around to gather bowls, thinking she had a good couple of days to gather up the energy for this dinner.

After Ethan left, Chloe figured she'd procrastinated long enough so she sat down at her desk to begin work for the day.

She had her ritual—Sari mug, which she turned so that the illustrated Breck was not visible—her Wonder Woman mouse pad, and her Game of Thrones background on her desktop Mac. Because Daenerys was awesome and so were her dragons. Chloe remembered when Samantha was alive, she'd ordered a latte from Starbucks and told the barista her name was Daenerys. The barista had written *Mother of Dragons* on her cup. Chloe and Samantha had laughed about it for weeks.

Chloe smiled at the memory, and ran her lip over the rim of her coffee cup.

Maybe she'd cosplay as Daenerys next year, or maybe Sansa, another character from Game of Thrones, because their dresses were gorgeous.

Chloe closed her eyes, the hair on her arms rising as she thought of Breck. It would be a long time before she forgot about him, before she could have another man touch her and not wish it was him.

For now, she took a sip of her coffee, opened up her email, and lost herself in her work. This was Chloe Talley at her finest, when she knew what the hell she was doing and did it with confidence. Code was black and white. Websites were secure or not. She recently left the software company she'd been working for and struck out as a freelancer, one of the best in the business, hired by banks and other institutions to penetrate their sites and find the weak spots.

She could do that, but the weak spots in her family? In her own life? Too numerous and complicated to figure out, like a cancer.

Except in Breck's arms. She'd sure as hell knew what she was doing then.

"Stop it, Chloe," she muttered to herself. "Forget him."

It didn't work.

Chapter Four

Grant sat at a table in Carrington's waiting for Ethan Talley, one of his friends and his new partner in ownership of *Gamers* Magazine.

For the last decade, Grant had owned Gamers with his best friend Austin Rivers, but Austin had decided to sell his ownership of the company, and Ethan had picked it up. Their new partnership gave Grant the excuse to get Ethan out of his penthouse. If the guy had his way, he'd stay locked in there all the time like a fucking hermit, playing video games and uploading his comments online.

Grant usually found an excuse to meet Ethan for dinner or some other type of social arrangement. He had met Ethan after his sister's death, when he was already a grouchy recluse, but Grant got the sense that Ethan hadn't always been like that. Sometimes Ethan told him stories of things he used to do, the places he used to travel, and it broke Grant's heart a little bit that Ethan did none of those things anymore.

Grant checked his phone. No text from Sydney so all must be okay. At a mature fourteen, she was old enough to be left home alone, plus, she'd shown herself to be responsible. She had a paper to write, so he knew she'd be busy until he got home.

The chair across from Grant scraped across the floor. He dropped his phone onto the table and looked up. Ethan sat across from him, pale blue eyes stark in the dimmed light of the restaurant.

"Nice of you to join me, Mr. Talley."

Ethan scowled. Sometimes Grant amused him but apparently this was not one of those times. "Traffic is a bitch."

To the point, that was Ethan. "So—"

"Whisky neat," Ethan ordered to the slim waiter who'd appeared at their table like a ghost.

Grant smiled at the guy, who was clearly startled by Ethan's abrupt order. "I'll take another Riesling, thanks."

The waiter vanished as quickly as he came. "Would it kill you to say thank you?" Grant asked.

Ethan ignored him. "My sister will be joining us."

Grant cocked his head. Ethan had two sisters, and only one was alive—the younger one—whom Grant had never met. "What's her name again?"

"Chloe," Ethan said.

"That's it. I was wondering why they seated us at a table for three."

"I called and changed the reservation."

"And what's the reason for your sister coming?"

The waiter returned with their drinks. Grant spun his glass on the ivory tablecloth while Ethan sipped his whiskey.

"She recently moved here. I"—he swallowed—"prefer her close. And she's a freelance software debugger so she can work anywhere, really."

"I didn't realize that's what she did."

"Yes, and she's very good. In high demand." Pride was evident in Ethan's voice.

Grant smiled. "That's wonderful."

"Since she's new to the area, I wanted to invite her out." Ethan paused and leaned forward, pinning Grant with a glare. "I had thought this didn't need to be said, but on second thought, I believe it does." Grant braced, not liking the ice shards in Ethan's eyes. "You touch my sister or look at her wrong and so help me God, I'll dismantle you."

Grant's stomach felt hollow, the force of Ethan's words stealing the breath from his lungs. Ethan was blunt and a little cold, but never threatening. "Jesus, Ethan. I'm not some caveman. I'm sure I can control myself from rutting against her in public."

"This isn't a joke, Grant."

"And I'm not laughing, but what is she, twenty-eight? You're not her protector." As soon as the words were out of his mouth, he wished he could shove them back in.

Ethan's entire body was one giant iceberg. Grant swore he could see his own breath in the chill.

"Don't tell me how to treat my family," the man said through gritted teeth.

Grant swallowed, his hackles immediately lowering. Ethan had already lost one sister, a death he blamed on himself. Sometimes Grant wondered how Ethan got out of bed every day with the weight of the guilt he'd placed on himself. Grant purposefully kept his gaze away from Ethan's neck and jaw, where the burn scars marred his skin. "You're right, Ethan. And I'm sorry. Either way, I'm looking forward to meeting Chloe."

Ethan didn't move for a minute, then slowly, his body seemed to thaw. He picked up his whiskey and drained it. "She's a little shy, but I'm very proud of her."

Heels clicking on the tile floor announced the arrival of shy-but-smart Chloe. Grant was midsip of his wine when he spotted her feet, encased in a pair of flesh-colored heels. Something about her ankles, the delicate bone. He flashed back to his princess, the way her breasts rose and fell as he licked at her ankle bone.

His stomach flipped.

He let his gaze travel up, his skin heating as he took in her knees, the way her thighs and hips shifted beneath the thin pencil skirt.

His fingers itched, remembering how they clutched Sari's hips in a bruising grip, how she'd arched her back and rode his cock.

Chloe's steps faltered, and Grant continued up, up, up until his gaze locked with hers.

His beautiful warrior princess's green eyes met his. And Grant almost spewed his wine across the table. Instead he swallowed it, and wished he had an excuse to take the glass and gulp down the rest of it until he couldn't remember a damn thing.

Sari was Chloe.

Two weeks ago, Grant had fucked Ethan's sister. He'd slapped her tits and licked her clit and stuck his cock in her mouth before he'd gripped her hair and rode her while she squirmed under him, begging him to fuck her harder.

He was going to hell. Although, hell might be better than what Ethan was going to do to him. Any minute now, Chloe was going to mention they'd met. Then the questions would start, and Grant wondered if he had his will all set, because his life was flashing before his eyes right now.

Except Chloe hadn't said a word. She stared at him, those green eyes completely terrified, unless he was reading her wrong. Her hair was short now, only brushing her shoulders in a cute bob. She swallowed, her voice trembling a little as she held out her hand. "Hello, I'm Chloe Talley."

Grant thought maybe she didn't recognize him, but there was a pleading in her eyes, and they were a little wet, her thick, dark lashes blinking rapidly.

He didn't know if she was doing this for herself or for him, but he was taking the life preserver she was throwing him. He'd clutch it to his chest until this fucking storm of a dinner was over.

He realized he was still sitting, staring at her like she was a circus freak. He discretely rubbed his sweaty palms on his pants and stood up. "Grant Osprey."

"Nice to meet you." Her voice was firmer now, and she sat down in the chair that Ethan had pulled out for her. Ever the vigilant brother, his gaze was ping-ponging back and forth between them.

Grant settled into his seat. "Nice to meet you, too. Ethan is happy to have you in town where he can practice his stalking tendencies."

She blushed prettily and ducked her head, the ends of her hair brushing her chin. She kind of looked like a Russian Bond Girl or something with that haircut. Fuck, this was bad. So bad. Why couldn't she be ugly? A bad lay? Something?

"It's nice to be back near family," she said. And Grant's heart pulsed in sympathy. The family had been through a lot with the death of their sister. Chloe didn't look any less broken up about it now.

Great, so not only did Grant want to fuck Ethan's sister, but he wanted to console her, too.

They were snug at a round table, the three of them. Chloe was so close the heat of her body warmed his side. The fabric of her skirt swished when she crossed and uncrossed her legs. The bracelets on her wrists jangled as she picked up the menu and looked over it.

When the waiter arrived again, he took Chloe's drink, as well as their food orders. She was quiet, sipping her merlot while Ethan talked about *Gamers*. Grant contributed to the conversation as best as he could, but half of his mind was on Chloe. She was quiet, almost too quiet. Where was his brazen princess? The one who was bold enough to approach him, who flirted shamelessly in a tavern, and who undressed in front of him with barely a hesitation?

The woman beside him now was soft-spoken and nervous. The waves of anxiety rolling off her were making *him* anxious. And Grant didn't get anxious.

There was a lull in the conversations as their food arrived. Grant knew he was playing with fire, but he couldn't stop poking it to see if it'd flare up. God, he was like a little kid with fireworks.

"So Ethan says you're one of the best at what you do?" he asked.

Chloe cut a small piece of chicken from the breast. "I-I have no trouble finding work."

Grant frowned, wondering why she had to hedge it like

that.

"She's just being Chloe. Modest as always. She's extremely talented," Ethan said. "She recently performed penetrative testing for a large bank in…where was that, Chloe?"

"Germany," she said.

"Germany," Ethan repeated. "She found a security breach that could have been very damaging."

Grant never pretended to be mature. Never ever. No matter how old he was. Ethan had just used penetrative testing in a sentence like that wasn't the funniest term in the world. Grant wanted to laugh, but instead, he decided to see how far he could push Chloe. Which was mean, but fuck it. She was acting so unlike the woman he'd met back at the convention, and it was driving him crazy. He placed an elbow on the table and his chin in his hands, rubbing his lips with his fingers. "Penetrative testing, huh?"

"I believe that's her specialty," Ethan said, completely clueless.

If looks could kill, Chloe would now be spitting on Grant's dead body.

But Grant had never been one to back off. "I might have to hire you for some penetrative testing." He lowered his voice, the innuendo unmistakable.

Ethan slammed a fist on the table. "Grant," he growled.

Grant immediately dropped his hands into his lap and faced Ethan. "Come on, you practically spoon-fed that to me."

"But this is my sister."

"I apologize, but you know better than to use words like that around me."

Ethan rolled his eyes. "Chloe, can you talk more about what you do? Use small words. Grant's operating on a twelve-year-old maturity level."

Chloe giggled, an honest to God giggle, and it was like music to Grant's ears. When he smiled at her, she cut off her laughter abruptly.

When she composed herself, she explained some of the jobs she'd recently completed, what companies she was contracted with, and what she excelled at. She lost herself a little, her hands waving enthusiastically, her face open and expressive. This was the woman he met back at the convention, a woman full of self-assurance and pride. She was beautiful like this, passionate about her job and her life. When she finally stopped talking, Ethan was beaming with pride, and Grant's mouth was hanging open.

He wanted her to keep talking, and it was painful to watch her take a sip of her wine and then begin her retreat back into herself. He wanted to dig a nail in and pull her back out.

"She's also an excellent cook," Ethan added.

Chloe smiled at her brother, and Grant saw the love in her expression. Man, what would it feel like for her to look at Grant like that? The thought surprised him, and he filed it away to deal with later. Maybe. Right now, Chloe wouldn't even meet his eyes. Grant raised his eyebrows. "Really? Do you bake?"

Chloe shrugged. Her eyes met his briefly, then skittered back to her plate. "A little."

This was painful, watching her struggle to engage in conversation with him. If he didn't know better, he'd say this was a different woman, but no, even in that short time they'd been together, he'd mapped this woman's body, studied her eyes. This was his princess, all right. His princess with all the fight knocked out of her.

Ethan dropped his napkin on the table beside his empty plate. "I need to use the restroom."

Grant watched his back as he made his way to the front of the restaurant where the restrooms were. When he turned to Chloe, he met her wide-eyed, terrified gaze. He was pretty sure his look mirrored hers.

Grant was fucked.

• • •

Chloe'd had a lot of nightmares in her life. Some weren't real. Some were.

And this... Well, this rated near the top, she was confident in confirming.

Breck was Grant. Grant was Breck.

And she was mortified.

She'd heard a little bit about Grant through Ethan. He was a smart businessman, and he loved his women. Women plural. The guy got around, apparently, and while she knew that she had just been another notch on Breck's bedpost, it rubbed her the wrong way to think she was a mark on Grant's.

This was why she didn't like to date, or socialize at all really. Because of awkward situations like the one she was in now, the one where Grant's blue eyes were glowing in the candlelight of the restaurant.

She had to admit that, during their meal, her mind had drifted to that night in the hotel room more times than she could count. He'd played her body like no man had ever done before. She'd experienced her first internal orgasm with him, for God's sake. She'd run home and researched it, because what he'd done to her had been beyond intense. Now that she was again in Grant's presence, her body tugged toward him, like he was gravity. She'd been so happy knowing that the last impression Breck/Grant had of her was the way she was as Sari. Knowing that Grant saw her now, as plain, simple, shy Chloe, was embarrassing. Of course they both knew they'd been playing parts. But it was under the assumption they'd never have to see each other without the armor. It was amazing how she'd taken her clothes off in front of this man and yet now—fully clothed—was when she'd never felt more naked.

Grant cleared his throat and opened his mouth and Chloe groaned. Because she didn't want to do this. She prayed silently that Ethan would hurry the hell up.

"I… It's good to see you again." Grant's hand drifted up and she would have flinched away if it was any other man. But she remembered his touch, and her body wanted to rub against him and purr like a cat. He brushed the bottom edge of her hair, and the movement of the strands tickled her scalp. "You cut your hair," he said softly, almost reverently. It was a simple way of acknowledging what they'd done.

She tucked it behind her ear. "It was really long."

Captain Obvious, reporting for duty.

He smiled. "I liked it long, but this suits you, too. You look really nice, Chloe."

Her name fell from his lips like dark chocolate. Seductive and sweet.

She took a large gulp of her wine. "So do you." She managed to make eye contact, watched as the candlelight gleamed on his golden hair, and she remembered his thick strands in her fingers. She clutched her skirt and kept her hands in her lap.

"So, you're Ethan's sister."

"And you're his business partner."

"Wow." Grant chuckled and rolled his eyes to the ceiling. "What are the fucking odds, huh?"

Chloe pursed her lips. "Well, there were roughly a couple thousand attendees, and I'm Ethan's only sister, so—"

Grant grinned at her. "You're actually trying to figure out the odds right now?"

She blushed and tried to hide her smile behind her fringe of hair. "You did ask, so…"

He chuckled. "I guess I did."

What was taking Ethan so damn long in the bathroom?

"Look, I—" Grant frowned. "Before you showed up, Ethan just about threatened to castrate me if I even looked at you weird, so it goes without saying that it's best he didn't find out what, uh, actually did happen. Already."

She was just as nervous as Grant. If Ethan knew what she did, how she got her pleasure, he'd probably lock her in his basement. Sure, she was a grown woman, but Ethan wasn't quite rational when it came to his remaining baby sister.

"Yes, this will just stay between us." She licked her lips and ran her finger over a drop of red wine she'd spilled on the tablecloth. "And in the past, obviously."

He leaned closer, the heat of his chest warming her bare arm. She closed her eyes, and then opened them when his breath tickled her ear. She stared ahead of her as he whispered, "Wish you wouldn't have left early though, Princess. I had plans for us."

His breath was still at her ear, raising the hairs on her

neck and if she turned her head, she'd touch those lips again, the ones she ached for since she kissed him last. She'd taste his mouth again, tangle her tongue with his talented one.

That was all it would take. One twist of her head. Instead, she sat frozen, staring straight ahead, until the heat of his body and his breath left her side.

"Sorry I took so long." Her brother's voice filtered through her haze of memories. She blinked and focused on him. "Saw an old acquaintance. Tried to duck out of it, but he saw me. I was even rude, but he persisted on catching up."

"God, forced into conversation in public. What's the world coming to these days?" Grant smirked.

Ethan scowled and Chloe snorted a laugh. Grant turned his head, catching her, so she tried to cover it up with a cough. It didn't work so well.

She reached up, fingering her earlobe, which still tingled from the vibration of Grant's voice, from his soft-spoken, *Princess*.

But that wasn't her anymore, that was another woman, one who stayed in that hotel room.

The conversation continued between the two men and Chloe concentrated on drinking. And eating. But mostly drinking.

Ethan had invited her out to meet his business partner, to engage her in his life. She was appreciative of that. He couldn't have known he was inviting her to a dinner with her last one-night stand.

By the time the check arrived, Chloe was exhausted from the constant churning of her mind, and she was also a little drunk. She hadn't remember ordering a bottle but there it was on the table in front of her, almost empty.

Oh boy.

Ethan signed the check and frowned at her as he clicked the pen down. "I'll take you home."

"I-I can take a cab—"

"I had one drink about forty-five minutes ago. I'll take you home."

She shut her mouth.

When they left the restaurant, Chloe followed Ethan, with Grant behind her, the heat of his gaze licking her back, butt, and legs.

She wanted this to be over. She wanted to be in her apartment, in her over-sized T-shirt and gaucho pants, curled up on the couch. At this point, she'd been *on* way longer than she was comfortable.

Grant and Ethan shook hands in the parking lot, and Grant turned to her. She took a step forward, and she wasn't sure if he intended to touch her, but no way could she handle that. She ducked her head, mumbled a good-bye, and took a step back.

Ethan led her to his car, and she risked one single glance over her shoulder. Grant stood in the parking lot, hands on his hips, watching them walk away. The slight breeze ruffled his hair and whipped up his tie. He was gorgeous, truly beautiful, and the knowledge that she'd had him for even one hour, was enough to ease the sour churning in her stomach.

After she was buckled into Ethan's Range Rover, he started the engine, frowning in her direction. "Are you okay, Chloe?"

"Fine," she answered, staring out the window.

"You seem tense."

"I guess."

"Are you stressed? Sleeping well? I noticed you didn't eat much at dinner—"

"Ethan, I'm just tired. It's been a long day."

She could tell he wanted to keep talking, but fortunately he fell silent. The vibration of the car lulled her to sleep, so that Ethan had to wake her by shaking her shoulder when they pulled into the parking lot of her apartment complex.

"I told you that you could stay with me," he said, patting her leg and squinting at the apartment building.

He'd drive them both crazy if she stayed at his house. "It's okay. I like having my own space. Thanks, though."

Ethan nodded and ran his hands over the steering wheel. "What'd you think of Grant?"

She paused with her hand on the door of the car. "Um, he seems nice."

Ethan looked at her. "He behaved himself while I was away from the table?"

Wish you wouldn't have left early, Princess. I had plans for us.

She cleared her throat. "Of course."

He nodded, seemingly satisfied with that answer. She figured it was time to make her exit. "Thanks for inviting me out tonight."

"You need anything, you call," he said.

She smiled. "Will do."

"Love you."

"Love you, too."

Ten minutes later, she was in her pajamas, a thick blanket wrapped around her, flipping through her Netflix queue. And she promised herself she'd forget about Grant and Breck, and continue her boring, drama-free life.

Chapter Five

Grant frowned at his daughter, who stood in front of him with her arms crossed over her chest, book bag on her back. "I told you I'll be fine."

It was Saturday morning and he was about to take Sydney to his parents' house. She stayed the weekend at their house every couple of months, and each time, she acted like he was going to throw a rager while she was gone and drink all the liquor.

"I made soup, so all you gotta do is heat it up," Sydney said, then narrowed her eyes. "And don't forget to put a piece of plastic wrap over top of it."

Right. Last time he'd heated up chili, it had exploded all over the microwave. Oops. "Yes, oh genius daughter."

"You going to be fine while I'm at Grandmom's and Granddad's?" she asked.

He threw up his hands. "I'm thirty-two and your father. I can handle a weekend by myself."

"Yeah but last time I spent the weekend there, you decided to retile the bathroom and we all remember how that turned out."

"My hand slipped," he groused, thinking back to the hole in the wall he'd had to patch.

Sydney rolled her eyes and hiked her book-bag strap higher on her shoulder.

"Don't forget the career fair on Monday. Work with your grandparents on your questions and answers, and I'll go over it all with you when you get home, okay?"

Sydney's face brightened. "I'm so excited. I heard they have several representatives from the STEM field there, so I hope I make a good first impression."

He ruffled the hair on top of her head before she shoved his hand away. "You'll be great. Have your outfit all picked out? You're supposed to dress like it's a real interview, right?"

She nodded.

"All right then. When I went to a career fair in high school, I found a mentor who I emailed with all through college. I'm sure you'll impress the hell out of everyone, and maybe you'll pick up a mentor, too."

Sydney bounced on her toes. "That'd be great."

"I'd offer Austin's services, but we all know that guy isn't so good at anything which requires talking and socializing." Sydney was interested in programming and while Austin had been a guide in the last couple of years, his daughter was eager to meet someone with another perspective.

"He's good with *me*."

Grant grinned. "Yeah, yeah. Okay let's get you over to your grandparents, okay?"

"Shotgun!" Sydney called when she ran out of the house.

Grant rolled his eyes as he locked the door behind him. She said that every time as if she wasn't the only passenger in the car when he drove. But then he thought about how she'd be getting her permit soon and shuddered.

After Grant dropped Sydney off with a kiss and a pat on her cheek, he drove around for a while. He could go to the gym, or sit in a coffee shop and read a book. He could go home and watch porn and jerk off.

Or... His mind drifted to Thursday night. Chloe with her short hair, that skirt. He couldn't believe she was the same girl who'd opened herself up to him in that hotel room. The Chloe last night was quiet and reserved. He wanted to know more about her, which was probably insane.

But it wasn't just that he was jonesing to see Chloe again, to be in her presence—he was awed at her close relationship with Ethan. Her brother adored her; it was easy to see. Grant knew he'd only seen the tip of the iceberg when it came to Chloe's personality. Ethan's devotion to her made Grant curious to know more.

And frankly, he wanted to know if that wanton princess act was real.

Twenty minutes later, Grant found himself in Ethan's driveway, listening to his engine cool down.

He bit his nail and jiggled his leg. He'd thought of calling Ethan last night and telling him the truth, but that would be a violation of Chloe's privacy. So instead, he had to find some way to weasel her number or address out of Ethan.

He stepped out of his car and took the porch stairs two at a time. He knocked on the door, but after a couple of minutes, he didn't get an answer.

Figuring Ethan was probably in the shower or something, Grant tested the door, which was unlocked. He opened it and walked right in.

"Ethan!" he called, wiping his feet on the mat. "Where are ya?"

He had to be there, right? The guy rarely went anywhere other than Grant's house, and Grant knew he wasn't there.

He heard a sound in the kitchen, a female voice, and he walked toward it, wondering if Ethan had a guest.

It didn't hit him until he was one foot in the kitchen that a female voice in Ethan's house would most likely be…

Chloe.

Because yep, there she was, scrubbing the countertop, earbuds in her ears, shaking her ass to music only she could hear. She wore short shorts and a thin, tight tank. He didn't know what she was doing here, cleaning Ethan's house, but Grant wasn't going to miss this show.

She sang softly, and Grant had to grin, because she was definitely singing Pink.

That said something about her, that she was here cleaning her brother's house on a Saturday when she could be at home doing something for herself. Everything about her so far showed a lot of heart and dammit if Grant didn't selfishly want some of that for himself.

He leaned against the doorframe and crossed his arms over his chest, enjoying watching her when she wasn't nervous or anxious. She was…happy, and free. And yes, it was voyeuristic, but dammit, she was beautiful with her face lit up, her now-short hair swinging about her face.

That is, until she spun around, spotted him, and screamed. She jerked the earbuds out of her ears and clapped a hand over her mouth, green eyes huge in her flushed face.

He didn't move, waiting to see how she'd react. The gears were turning in her head, something working behind her eyes. Slowly, she lowered her hand, her fingers grazing her neck, until her palm rested on her upper chest.

Grant figured this could go one of several ways. She could ignore him. She could tell him to leave. They could engage in super awkward, weeks-after-dirty-hotel-sex conversation until Ethan got back.

Or they could fuck again.

He watched her, studying her body language. Her lips were parted, gaze roaming his face and chest. If he hadn't seen her aroused before, he wouldn't have noticed. But he had seen her, naked and so fucking needy.

As Sari, as his princess, she'd been bold, unafraid to voice what she wanted. There'd been no shyness to Sari, no hesitation to seek pleasure, no embarrassment for wanting a simple human need. In a role, Chloe had been dynamic; she'd been able to say what she wanted. And maybe he was reading her wrong there in the kitchen, but if he was right, she wasn't opposed to Grant touching her again.

Time to see if his wanton princess wanted to come out and play.

This could crash and burn in epic failure. Grant was a thirty-two-year-old man and this was probably a horrible idea. But he couldn't get Chloe's green eyes out of his head, the way she kissed him, the way she moved under his palms. And, fuck, the way she tasted... So, he took a deep breath and went for it, knowing this could completely end in Ethan ripping out his heart like in that Indiana Jones movie.

Grant tipped up his lips and narrowed his eyes, adopting

the air of a domineering businessman. "I thought I told you that I wanted the entire house finished by the time I got back. I'm not paying you to dance around the kitchen."

Her chest rose and fell with deep breaths, and Grant waited, on fucking pins and needles to see if she'd play along.

The only sound was the refrigerator kicking on, and he was about to laugh, and tell her he was joking, when her voice, small but gaining power, said, "But, sir, you're home early."

That *sir* went right to his cock.

He took a step toward her, smiling when she backed up into the counter behind her. "I'm only a half an hour early, and you have a lot more than half an hour of work to do. What's your excuse?"

Her lips parted. "I—"

He stepped into her space, plucking her iPod from the waistband of her pants, setting it on the counter along with her earbuds. Her eyes fluttered closed.

"Yes, Sara?" he questioned, hands on either side of her, pinning her in. The name he made up was close enough to Sari that he figured he'd remember it.

She opened her eyes, and he stared into the swirling green pool of her irises. She was in the role now; he could feel it. "I'm sorry but I took a nap in your bed."

Jesus, his cock twitched and he shifted, so the front of his jeans brushed her thigh. "You napped in my bed?"

She bit her lip and nodded. "I know, I w-was bad."

God, he was going to come in his pants. He ran a hand along the outside of her thigh, teasing the skin under the hem of her shorts. "Is that all you did? Sleep?"

She shook her head.

"No? What did you do in my bed?"

"I-I touched myself."

Her whisper was a lick across his balls. With a grip on her biceps, he spun her around, so she faced the counter. She gripped it with a cry, but didn't struggle. Instead, she threw her head back and pushed out her ass.

He took the invitation for what it was. He lowered her shorts along with her panties, hooking the fabric under the cheeks of her ass.

He smoothed a hand over it, and reveled in the small moan she made in the back of her throat. "You know I need to punish you, right?"

She nodded, her hair bobbing.

"I'll go easy on you if you're truthful with me."

"Okay, sir."

He squeezed one cheek, then let it go, watching as the blood rushed back to the white areas made by his fingers. "What did you think about when you touched yourself?"

The hesitation was for effect, he knew it. What a little actress she was. She looked at him over her shoulder, smiling coyly and blinking under her lashes. "You, sir. I thought about you and your huge cock."

The first smack was harder than he intended, because fuck, she brought him to the edge. That voice, that look, that ass that reared back into his palm, begging to be slapped. "So bad, Princess," he murmured into her ear, rubbing the area he'd marked, needing to get control. "You're so bad."

"So bad," she echoed, rolling her hips, grinding against the counter. "I need to be punished, sir."

He smacked her again, opposite cheek, then began to alternate as he gained a steady rhythm. He was about to burst in his jeans, his cock straining against the zipper but at least he'd been able to gain control of his arm. He wanted to mark her, just a little bit, but not bruise.

Her skin was hot, red, and tight under his palm and goddamn, what he wouldn't have done at that moment to feel that hot ass against his skin as he gripped her hips and thrust into her. But next time he fucked her—and Grant vowed, there would be a goddamn next time—they were doing it face to face. Because he wanted those large tits bouncing in his face, her nipples brushing his lips.

But now, she needed him, his princess. She was right on the edge, he could tell by the way her breath came in pants, the way her arms trembled where she gripped the counter. He slid his hand down the seam of her ass, until he reached the slick walls of her pussy. He immediately plunged his fingers inside of her, feeling her contract around them. She cried out and ground against him.

He gripped her chin, rearing her head back and smashed his forehead to her temple. "That's it, Princess. Ride my fingers." She was letting herself go, so un-self-conscious, and it was beautiful. "*This* is the girl I've been missing. The one who comes hard for me."

Her breath broke on a sob and he angled his hand, so a finger pressed against her clit, rubbing and swirling and pinching until she was done for. She pulsed against his hand, her cries echoing throughout the kitchen. And he smiled as his princess came apart.

Every instinct in him screamed to unzip his jeans, to relieve this pressure in his balls and take her right then, right there in Ethan's kitchen.

And that was the problem. This was Ethan's house.

This was Ethan's sister. And there he was, with a bare-assed Chloe, his hand still buried inside of her, while she caught her breath from the orgasm he'd just wrung out of her, little whimpers escaping her throat.

God, what was it about her? He was fucking addicted to her body, to the sounds she made when she came, to the look in her eyes when she was aroused. But if Ethan ever found out…

"Chloe, we need to talk," he said in her ear.

And just like that, her body stiffened. She took a giant step to the side, so his fingers slipped from her. She pulled up her panties and shorts, and ran her hands through her hair. She was shaking, her whole body trembling. He didn't know how to fix this, how to get back to when she was putty in his hands.

"Chloe—"

"You need to go before Ethan gets home." She'd picked up her sponge and was back to scrubbing the countertops. Completely ignoring him like he hadn't just had a part of his body inside of hers.

"Chloe, Jesus Christ. We *have* to talk about this. I mean, we both wanted that, and it happened, and I don't see why it can't happen again—"

She whirled to face him, green eyes terrified. "No. No, it can't happen again."

He stared at her. "Uh, well you said that last time and here we are, in post-orgasmic-fucking-bliss. Well, at least one of us."

At least a glimmer of sympathy flitted across her face as her gaze flicked to the front of his pants. "Look, I—"

The front door opened, effectively freezing them both.

"Grant? Chloe?" Ethan called.

Chloe's eyes were huge, and all Grant could do was stand there, the smell of her still on his fingers. He was a grown-ass man and this was some teenage bullshit. "Guess Daddy's home," he muttered.

...

She'd gone insane. There was really no other rational explanation for why she'd let Grant spank her and finger-bang her in Ethan's kitchen.

No, *let* wasn't the right word. God, she'd asked for it, *begged* for it.

Damn Grant, with his perfect hair and beautiful eyes and talented fingers. *Damn* him. He'd known exactly what she'd needed to let go, to give in to her body's cravings. He gave her a role and she'd slipped right into it. She'd always had a bad maid fantasy. She had a lot of fantasies like that, but hell if she'd ever acted one out. This fantasy now could have used a better outfit, and a feather duster. Maybe one of those little caps? That would have really done the fantasy justice. She had to wing it a little without her props.

Now here she stood, the skin between her legs wet, a hollow feeling where Grant's fingers had been, and the sound of her brother's footsteps getting closer.

Grant was tense, the bulge in his pants less now, but he was surely still uncomfortable.

Ethan walked into the kitchen, frowning when he spotted them. "Chloe, I told you that you didn't have to clean. I have a housekeeper."

She nearly swallowed her tongue.

Ethan dropped a bag of groceries on the counter and turned to Grant, raising his eyebrows. "What are you doing here? I saw your car outside."

Grant shrugged, shoving his hands in his jeans. "Just wanted to say hi."

Chloe decided that was her cue to leave. She'd come over that morning, unwilling to sit in her apartment by herself because she couldn't get Grant out of her head. And all that did was lead her right into his hands. His very capable hands.

She dropped the sponge in the sink and grabbed her iPod off the counter. "Well, uh, I'll leave you two then."

She walked by Ethan, who protested. "You don't have to leave —"

"I have some errands to run," she lied. "Have a great Saturday." She dropped a kiss on his cheek.

"Thanks for cleaning," he said.

When she'd showed up, he hadn't been home, so she'd busied herself, even though his kitchen was damn near spotless. As she walked down the hallway, she glanced over her shoulder. Ethan's back was to her as he put away groceries and Grant stood watching her, a look of longing on his face that socked her in the gut.

She quickly turned around, and left the house, jogging to her car parked at the curb.

But when she got inside, she didn't start it. Instead she gripped the steering wheel with white knuckles.

Grant was charming, and funny, and when he was around, when his lips were whispering dirty words in her ear, she forgot about everything but the pleasure they could wring from each other.

So far, he was willing to play her game, let her act a role, and for that she was grateful. Because Chloe? Chloe didn't bite her lip coyly, or react like a wanton when her ass was slapped.

No, he didn't want Chloe. He wanted Sari. And Sara.

She could give him that.

And really, after all she'd been through, didn't she deserve that escape? They could keep it from Ethan. Just a couple more times. Surely, she'd start craving Grant less eventually, right?

Without thinking too much about it, she grabbed a scrap of paper and a pen, scribbling some words on it, her cheeks heating as she thought about what he'd think when he read it.

Then she glanced quickly at Ethan's house. Seeing no movement in the front windows, she jumped out of her car and dashed to Grant's. After a moment of hesitation, she slipped the piece of paper under his windshield wiper and then ran back to her car. When she was safely behind her wheel, turning the ignition, she had a moment of indecision. She should run back, take out that piece of paper, and forget all about Grant.

And she thought about it, but then she saw the curtain move in Ethan's front window. So she slammed the car into gear and sped off.

She was still breathing hard when she parked in front of her apartment complex. She glanced at her dashboard clock. Approximately ten hours until she asked Grant to meet her. Ten hours to agonize over her decision with no way to tell him she was backing out. The thought of standing him up sat like lead in her stomach. He didn't deserve that. He'd done everything she asked of him—and then some. He'd given her a role to play, enabling her to give in to her desire. And he still wanted her, despite the way she'd spurned him afterward.

When she was safely in her house, she thought about cooking one of several new dishes she'd been meaning to try, something to take her mind off what was to come. But the last time she'd cooked distracted, she'd melted a plastic spoon, so maybe that wasn't such a good idea.

Her eyes strayed to the lone picture she'd taped on her refrigerator. Chloe, Samantha, and Ethan stood, arms around each other, grinning like fools in front of Lake Erie, where they'd taken a vacation on Ethan's dime. The three of them, along with their parents, rented a house and spent an entire week together.

It'd been the last time they'd been a family of five. Because a week later, Samantha was dead and Ethan was in the hospital suffering from third-degree burns to his chest and neck.

She closed her eyes and turned away from the picture, thinking she should take it down rather than be reminded of when smiles had come easy.

That was in the past, and tonight, she had a role to play. One she'd been dying to play for a while. And she had the perfect dress for it.

Chapter Six

This was insanity.

Grant ran his hand over the pocket of his pants, comforted in the crinkle of paper he felt there. The club music was loud, the base pounding the floor beneath his shoes. The crowd was drunk already at ten at night. He couldn't imagine what this placed looked like at last call.

The lights were so dim, he could barely see his hands in front of his face, but he figured that was the idea. No one did the things people were doing on the dance floor with all the lights on.

He shifted uncomfortably, checking his watch. Chloe was half an hour late, and he was starting to wonder if she'd changed her mind, or if this was all a joke.

He fished in his pocket for the slip of paper and squinted at the scrawled handwriting, tilting it toward a low light behind the bar where he stood.

Bax's Club
9:30 PM
Sara will be in the black dress. She owes you.

Just like when he'd found the note on his car, his cock twitched. He'd remembered what she'd looked like on the edge of the bed in that hotel room weeks ago, full lips stretched around him. He wanted that again, and then he wanted those legs wrapped around him as he pounded her into the wall.

He was surprised as hell that she prompted this. In Ethan's kitchen, she'd looked scared, a hint of vulnerability creeping in when she firmly told him this wouldn't happen again. But here they were, about to play out the rest of their sir-maid fantasy. Or at least, he was here. Chloe had yet to show.

And fuck if Grant couldn't wait. He shoved the note back into his pants pocket and downed the rest of his rum and Coke. As he set the empty glass on the bar, a pair of fingers slipped through his belt buckle and tugged.

He whirled around, prepared to tell whomever was touching him that he was waiting for someone.

But his mouth went dry and fell open when he stared into Chloe's green eyes. The colored light behind the bar gave them an eerie, inhuman look. She'd lined them thickly with eyeliner and her lips were a bright red.

He'd seen a lot of little black dresses in his life, but none even came close to the scrap of material Chloe was wearing. Her breasts were plumped up, spilling out over the top. He balled his fists when all he wanted to do was pull down the neckline, let those breasts pop out so he could see her pretty pink nipples.

The dress was skintight and barely covered her ass. It shimmered in the rotating strobe light of the DJ booth, the material appearing to have a metallic sheen. Most of her gorgeous thighs were bared to his gaze. He homed in on those delicate anklebones that intrigued him so, showed off in a pair of silver stilettos.

Her hair was straight, her bangs brushing along the top of her long black lashes, and she clutched a small red bag.

He met her emerald gaze again, having a hard time reconciling this siren with the meek woman he'd eaten dinner with earlier in the week.

She was the same though, he knew. And this was her idea. And he was a sucker for letting her think she could hide from him, but if role-playing was the only way he could get close to her, he'd take it. For now.

Her palm cupped him through his pants, and he leaned down so she could speak in his ear. "Thought about you all day, sir. How would you like to be repaid for the time I wasted?"

He was growing in her hand, hardening as she stroked him through the material. "I expect payment to be made on your knees, Sara."

Her breath caught in his ear, and then a small hand slipped in his. He was led away from the bar, away from the dance floor, and down a hallway. They walked past the bathrooms and he thought about questioning her, but he was too mesmerized by the way her ass moved in front of him, the sound of her heels clicking on the tile floor, as she led him down one dark hallway after another.

He wanted to leave breadcrumbs in their wake to show

him the way back. Although something told him, after this night, he might never find his way back to the way things were.

And that didn't scare him like it should have. Instead, he followed this woman, this beautiful woman who confused him and turned him on. Who responded so well to his hands and tongue and cock.

He followed her because in that moment, there was no other option in his mind.

She tested a couple of doors, jiggling the knobs until she found one that gave way. She pulled him inside and shut the door behind them, pushing him backward until his shoulders touched the door.

A light flickered on and he blinked at the source of it, which was a naked bulb screwed into a ceiling fixture. Chloe stood before him, nipping at his jawline. He grabbed the back of her head firmly and brought her mouth to his. He bit her lips and licked into her mouth. She made small, greedy moans, and rolled her hips against him as her hands pushed at his jacket.

He pulled out of the kiss and tugged off his jacket quickly, dropping it on the floor at her feet. "Knees," was all he said.

The flush on her face extended down to the tops of her breasts. She visibly shuddered at his command, and while meeting his gaze, slowly lowered to her knees.

She didn't take her eyes off his as she flicked open the button of his suit pants, lowered the zipper, and pulled out his cock. He'd gone commando tonight, just for her.

Her gaze was on his cock now and so was his, watching her hand stroke him as her other hand teased his balls with light brushes of her fingertips. He spread his legs wider. "Go on and suck it."

She descended slowly, pressing the tip of his cock against her closed lips, then slowly opening them, keeping a seal around his shaft as she descended to the root.

It was exquisite, this slow torture, the heat, the wetness. Her tongue pressed against his tip, swirling, dipping into the slit and he moaned, clutching her hair in his fist and bucking slightly into her throat.

She gagged and he let her pull back, off his cock, only to dip her head and suck one of his balls into her mouth.

Her tongue prodded at the thin skin, and he thunked his head back onto the door, closing his eyes, as she paid equal treatment to his other ball, then lapping at the skin between them.

"Fuck," he muttered, unable to form any other proper words as she once again took his cock in her mouth on that slow descent, this time hollowing out her cheeks on the way back, sucking hard.

His balls were already drawing up tight, his orgasm tickling his spine. But this wouldn't do. He'd vowed to fuck her good and proper, face-to-face, so he could see into those emerald eyes while he was inside of her.

With a tug on her hair, he pulled her off his cock. She resisted, mouth open, like she couldn't wait to get him back in her mouth, but he growled, and her eyes shot to his.

"Stand up," he ordered, and she gathered her feet under her, rising to her full height. He spun them around so her back was to the door, and took her mouth again, tasting the saltiness of his skin on her tongue.

Her hands brushed his cock but he grabbed her wrists

and slammed them on either side of her head. "Keep 'em there," he grunted. "I'm going to take my time with this body as my payment, and you're going to let me, understand?"

She bit her lip and nodded.

...

Chloe was so turned on, she was nearly out of her mind. She could still taste Grant's cock in her mouth, the smooth skin surrounding the hardness that she could have sucked on all night. She wanted to taste him as he came, spilling into her mouth.

Some day. Because she had at least a modicum of sense to realize she was addicted to sex with the man.

His eyes were in shadow from the light over his head, but she could see the shining blue irises dropping to her chest. He licked his lips, hooked one finger in the neckline of her strapless dress, and tugged it down.

Her breasts fell out, full and aching, her nipples already hard. She gasped as the cool air of the room wafted over her sensitive skin. Her hands came off the door beside her head for an instant, before she remembered Grant's order and placed them back.

Grant's hips were pressed against hers, pinning her to the door. He palmed each breast, jiggling them. She'd never met a man who was as into breasts as Grant was, but she didn't mind. She had plenty to go around and her nipples had always been ultra-sensitive, like they were a line directly to her G-spot.

"I've been thinking about these gorgeous tits," he said, almost reverently, flicking his thumbs over the nipples. "They feel so good in my hands, but I bet they'd feel better in my mouth, huh, Princess?"

She rocked her hips into his. "Please."

He squeezed the flesh in his hands. "Yeah? Do you want me to suck them?"

"Yes," she sobbed.

"Beg me," his voice was low. "Beg me to suck them."

She hesitated. Chloe, of course, would never do that. But she was Sara now. She was Grant's slutty maid who touched herself, who came in Grant's bed. And she needed to repay him for the time she should have been working.

"Please," she said breathlessly. "Please suck on my tits, sir."

He cursed and then his hands were on the back of her thighs, hauling her off her feet. She wrapped her legs around his waist and locked her ankles at his back. Grant's face was already between her breasts, his tongue licking a path up the inside of one and down the inside of the other. Then a nipple was in his mouth and he was sucking, sucking so hard that she swore she'd be bruised tomorrow. But what a souvenir, to have hickeys all over the soft skin of her breasts from Grant's talented mouth.

"So fucking good," he murmured against her skin as he moved on to the other nipple, adding teeth and a tongue swirl.

He was thrusting against her, his bare cock rubbing along her bare flesh. She'd worn no panties, which she knew was a risk, but she hadn't intended to be in public in the club long.

Her arousal slicked his cock between her folds, and Grant raised his head, lips red and wet from his attention to her breasts. "Jesus, you're not wearing anything under this dress?"

She shook her head.

Grant's lips curled. "So hungry for this cock, you went bare?"

Her answer was to grind into him, gripping the hair at the base of his neck. Because she was hungry. Starving. She wanted him so bad, she couldn't even speak. Her hips moved mindlessly, her inner muscles clenching, begging for him to plunge inside of her.

A hand left her ass and then she heard the crinkle of a condom wrapper. He rolled it on his cock, his other still holding her up. She helped by holding onto his shoulders and waist.

"I've been dreaming about fucking you like this. You ready?"

"Fuck me," she said.

His lips twisted cruelly. He pulled her legs apart farther, and lowered her onto his cock with a grunt.

She was so slick, she sank right onto him with no resistance. She shoved her face into his neck, moaning as he filled her.

"Lean back, Princess. I want to watch these tits while I fuck you against this door."

His mouth was going to drive her to insanity. She swallowed and pushed back, bracing herself on his shoulders, and let her head rest on the door. His gaze was on her breasts. He flicked the nipple of each one with that long, talented tongue. Then he smiled, and began to thrust.

The door banged on its hinges, the sound unmistakable to anyone walking by what they were doing.

Her large breasts bounced obscenely in Grant's face and he watched them, licking his lips and occasionally drawing a nipple into his mouth, sucking and biting.

At this angle, he hit her clit with every thrust, not enough to come, but enough for her to feel her orgasm building, that telltale prickle in her toes.

"Oh my God." She arched her back, pushing her breasts into Grant's face further. She placed a hand on the back of his head, urging him to draw her into his mouth. Which he did eagerly, sucking on her beaded tips.

"Reach down and play with your clit," he said, pulling back and watching where his cock entered her body.

She ran a hand down over her breasts, down her stomach, and pinched her clit, swirling it with the pad of her middle finger. "I'm close."

"Yeah? Me, too, Princess." He was breathing hard, his chest heaving. She realized he was fully clothed, and her dress was merely a strip of fabric under her breasts.

That was all it took, that image of a suited man fucking her mostly naked body, to send her into orbit. She threw her head back and cried out, the orgasm rocketing through her, curling her toes.

Grant continued to thrust, riding out her orgasm, until he too followed her with a whispered, "Princess," falling from his lips.

She clung to him, not trusting her legs to support her. He slowly let her down, helping her stand on wobbly legs.

He pulled her dress up over her breasts carefully, lovingly, before dropping to his knees.

"What—" she began.

He laid a hand on her stomach, met her eyes, and then

licked her soaked skin. The breath left her lungs in a rush as he took his time with her slick folds and inner thighs.

Then he rose and pressed his lips to hers so she tasted herself. "I've been waiting to get a taste of you again," he said softly.

For a moment, she wondered if she'd come again, just from those words. Although, it was a reminder that this wasn't the first time they'd been together. She didn't want to think about that. She had to keep up the role and not slip. Because she wanted this. She wanted Grant, and she couldn't do it as Chloe. Hell, Grant wouldn't *want* her as Chloe. Chloe was quiet and meek, introverted and nerdy. She let everyone down, and he'd be no exception once he realized she wasn't the fun, sexually liberated girl he thought she was.

No, the role was all she could afford to give him.

She straightened her skirt and looked up at him through her lashes. "So, was this payment sufficient?"

He blinked, like he needed a minute to figure out what she was referring to. He smiled then, but it didn't reach his eyes. "Yeah, yeah, it's sufficient."

She reached for the doorknob and turned it. "Great, it won't happen again, then, sir."

He jerked a thumb toward the door. "I was, uh, going to stay and have a drink or two, if—"

She shook her head, cutting him off. No. No. That wasn't what this was. It wasn't a date or a chat. This was sex. Dirty, incredibly fulfilling sex, and that's where it would stay. She needed to get home before she turned into a pumpkin...or rather, *Chloe*. With glasses, gaucho pants, and a worn T-shirt that said, *Talk Nerdy to Me*.

"I need to get home," she said, hoping he didn't push it.

Something flitted across his face, and then he reached out and grabbed her wrist before she could leave the closet. He dug into his pocket and pulled out a slip of paper, pressing it into her hand.

She curled her fingers around it.

He cleared his throat and scratched his head, one of the first times she saw him unsure. "Then, uh, yeah. Be sure it doesn't happen again."

She nodded and slipped out of the door, not looking back once as she left the club.

Chapter Seven

Chloe twisted her fingers together, cursing her brother under her breath as she stood in front of a high school.

A high school.

She loved classes and books and projects. School-supply shopping was like Christmas. But the rest of school…the socializing, the social structure, the—she shuddered—school dances, were not enjoyable. The opposite of enjoyable, actually, not unlike how she imagined it would feel if her intestines were pulled out through her belly button.

She needed to stop watching horror movies.

Conway Ridge High School was okay-looking, she guessed, as far as high schools went. The front walk had some sort of artsy sculpture that looked like a giant paper clip and the brick entrance seemed fairly modern.

Ethan had asked her to participate in a career day. Why, she wasn't sure, because obviously the social skills this took weren't her forte. He said the school routinely sent out letters asking professionals in the area to help. He'd turned them down for years now and felt guilty about it. But apparently not guilty enough for him to do this. Oh no, he'd sent her like a sacrificial lamb.

Samantha would have been amazing at this. She knew how to act in front of people, how to be a role model. Chloe, on the other hand, not so much. She couldn't even be the person she needed to be for her family; how was she going to be that person for some teenager?

Well, there was nothing for it now. The only problem was that her mind was still two days behind her body, back in Saturday night when she'd been screwed against a door in a back room at the club. Even now, just thinking about it warmed her belly. How the hell was she supposed to get through today? Around kids and students when all she could think about was Grant's tongue and hands and cock?

She needed a cold shower.

Instead, she took a deep breath, pushing the memories aside and focusing on the present, and tried to think mature, responsible thoughts. As she walked to the front door, the *click* of her heels echoed off the brick of the building. She'd worn the same pair of nude-colored heels she'd worn to dinner with her brother and Grant, along with a tan skirt with a pale pink sweater. Her makeup was even done, which she thought she should get an award for. Sari wore makeup, but Chloe? Not so much.

She pressed a button, and once she announced her name and her purpose, she was buzzed inside. Her first stop was the front office, where she was given a visitor's badge and was introduced to a red-haired teenage girl with a smile full of braces. The memories from high school were battering

Chloe's brain. Was there anything worse than braces, really?

"Hi, I'm Kendall," the girl said in a nervous voice, holding out her hand. She stood straight and proud as the secretary explained to Chloe that the brightest and most well-behaved students were handpicked to be guides for the visiting professionals. Kendall wore a pair of khakis, a button-down shirt, and clunky dress shoes. Some of it was ill-fitting and Chloe's heart cracked a little. When she was younger, she used to wish she had a younger brother or sister to dote on. So she had a soft spot in her heart for kids, especially girls. She smiled and shook the girl's hand. "Hello, Kendall, I'm Chloe Talley."

Kendall brightened further. "I'm going to lead you to the gymnasium, where the career fair will be held. Would you like any coffee or water?" she gestured to a table behind her, which held refreshments.

"Just a bottle of water is fine," Chloe said.

Kendall seemed to be thrilled that she could provide one.

Chloe followed the teenager out of the office while Kendall chattered on about what the school mascot was (a wildcat), what sports they excelled at (swimming, diving, and girls' soccer until the star forward tore her ACL). Classes for the day had started fifteen minutes ago, so the hallway was quiet except for a couple of other professionals led by teenagers.

The gymnasium was large, the bleachers rolled back against the wall, the floor dotted with dozens of tables. Some mentors were already seated, and Chloe nodded to those she passed as Kendall led her to a table. And there was her name, in thick black letters on a tented piece of paper—Chloe Talley, Software Analyst.

She ran her finger along the edge, while Kendall explained that the room was sectioned into fields of study. Chloe was among the STEM professionals and it didn't surprise her that the tables in her area were occupied by men. All except her.

That made her chest fill a little with pride, an unfamiliar feeling she hadn't had since…well maybe since she'd graduated summa cum laude from her university. Back then she'd been in classes with mostly men. Being the lone vagina in a room wasn't foreign to her, and she'd learned to prove her worth by keeping her head down and working hard.

It was amazing how graduating at the head of her major shut the mouths of her misogynistic peers.

"I need to head back to the office, is there anything else I can do for you, Miss Talley?" Kendall asked.

Chloe shook her head. "No, but thank you very much. You've been a wonderful host."

Kendall beamed and when she walked away, Chloe noticed it was with her head back, shoulders straight.

Chloe sat down and pulled the paperwork out of her bag that the school had sent ahead of time. There was a list of questions the students had been prepped on that she was to ask, and the rest she was to improvise. Hating to be unprepared, Chloe had made notes all over the page, changing the words of some questions and adding many of her own that she didn't want to forget to ask.

She'd have fifteen minutes with six students to discuss her field. Those students had been given a list of the occupations of the professionals coming, and they'd chosen who they wanted to meet. Today's career fair was for the freshman and sophomores.

A bell rang, signaling the end of classes, and Chloe knew that meant the students would be here soon. She was nervous as hell, and hoped she managed to do something to help these kids today.

She opened her water and took a sip, then checked her phone. Ethan had texted, *Good Luck.*

You owe me, she texted back.

Always, he answered.

She frowned, wondering what that meant, but then the doors to the gym were opened and students began to line up behind teachers with clipboards.

The first three students were boys. One seemed genuinely interested. He bobbed his head enthusiastically when he talked, so his glasses slipped down his nose, causing him to adorably shove them back up. One seemed bored as hell and she got the impression he was being forced to consider this career because of his parents, and the other was painfully shy, talking in a voice so quiet, she had to ask him to repeat himself. Which made her feel old, like she needed a hearing aid when she wasn't even thirty.

The fourth student was a girl, who wore a brilliant smile and a pretty sweater dress. Her hair was a dirty blond, braided so that the end rested at the front of her shoulder. Her blue eyes crinkled as she sat down, and Chloe felt a momentary pang of something familiar, but pushed it aside.

"Hello, I'm Sydney," the girl said.

Chloe smiled. "Hi, Sydney, I'm Chloe Talley."

The girl's eyes flicked to Chloe's name tag on the desk. "I like your name." Then she flushed and her fingers fluttered at the end of her braid, and then she slapped her hand back down into her lap. "Sorry, that was kind of dumb to say. I'm nervous."

The girl's admission of nerves was so honest, that Chloe had a hard time not hugging her. Instead, she adopted the least threatening posture she could. "I'm nervous too, actually."

Sydney focused on Chloe. "Really?"

She wanted to be something for this girl, something… worthwhile. Sydney was bright and full of energy and damn, maybe Chloe could get it together for an hour to make a positive impact on this girl's life. "Yeah, of course. I'm used to speaking to my computer all day and it doesn't talk back. I think this is really brave of you to participate in this career day."

Sydney clearly liked the praise; her smile was huge. "Yeah," she said, clearly gaining confidence. "I mean, we didn't have to, but I signed up."

"See?" Chloe held out her hands. "You're one step ahead." Chloe leaned in and lowered her voice. "And you know what I do when I'm nervous?"

Sydney leaned in, her face open in wonder, like Chloe was about to tell her the meaning of life. "What?"

"I picture people in their pajamas."

Sydney wrinkled her nose and giggled. "Pajamas?"

"Yep. Pajamas."

"That sounds like something my dad would say."

"Well, then, I'm sure your father is a smart man."

Sydney straightened her back. "He's so super-smart. He's the reason I'm interested in computer science."

Now they were getting somewhere. Chloe waved her hand. "Great, so tell me more about why you're interested in this industry and then I'll ask you questions and you can ask me some. Sound good?"

Sydney nodded eagerly. And the next ten minutes were spent with a talkative, full-of-life Sydney. Chloe enjoyed talking to the bright girl, hearing her hopes and dreams. She reminded her a little of herself when she was that age. So full of ideas, the future bright.

Chloe basked in the girl's enthusiasm, hoping a little rubbed off on her.

When their time was up, Chloe didn't want to let the girl go, and Sydney seemed to share the feeling. "So, if this isn't okay, you can let me know, but I have more questions to ask and I'm wondering if we could do this again?"

Chloe reached into her bag and handed Sydney her business card. "My email is on there, which is the best way to reach me. And if you want to meet in person, that's fine. I'd just ask that a parent is present since it won't be supervised by the school."

Sydney held the business card in her hand like it was gold, running her finger over the letters. In that moment, Chloe was glad she splurged for the raised print.

"Yes, that's fine. I'll ask my dad. Thank you so much. I really enjoyed meeting you!" This girl was all exclamation points and energy.

Chloe smiled. "Of course, and it was wonderful meeting you, Sydney. Keep up the good work in school."

"Will do!" Sydney skipped off, and Chloe thought maybe, just maybe she wasn't such a failure after all.

· · ·

Grant shook the hand of Aaron Shivers, the head of the advertising team of one of the largest technology security firms in the country—Erotech. He grinned big, hoping it wasn't bordering on maniacal, because it had taken him a lot of coffee and a bonus Red Bull to be coherent for this meeting.

A very important meeting.

Which he was pretty sure he'd pulled off thanks to some charm, mild professionalism, and good old-fashioned luck.

Mr. Shivers shook his hand firmly back and smiled. "Thanks a lot for meeting with us Mr. Osprey. My teenage daughter will be thrilled to hear I've met you. She's quite the gamer."

"Bring her by sometime," Grant said cheerfully, ignoring Marley Lake's raised eyebrows from her position in the corner. "We can always show her around. In fact, she could shadow one of my editors if she'd like for a career-day opportunity."

Oh man, he was really pouring it on thick, but he wanted this account. His main goal this year was to get larger advertisers for the magazine. He had a sales team, but for the larger accounts, he liked to take the lead position.

Good thing Mr. Shivers was eating it up. "Sounds great. I'll let her know. My team and I are going to review everything we talked about today and we'll be in touch on how we want to proceed."

Grant hoped it involved a big check but he wasn't going to say that. "Sounds great. And don't forget to tell your daughter about that tip I told you in *Minecraft*."

Mr. Shivers laughed. "I'll never see her again. She'll be playing nonstop."

"Ah," Grant said with a wink. "Then I guess you'll have

to play, too."

"Ugh." Mr. Shivers clapped him on the shoulder. "You take care and I'll be in touch."

Once Mr. Shivers and his team left, Grant collapsed into his chair and rubbed his forehead, a headache from all the caffeine beginning to form.

Marley, the newly appointed assistant editor at Gamers, sank down into the chair beside him, the leather creaking as she crossed her legs. "I don't know how you do it," she said.

"Do what?" he mumbled. "Do we have any Advil?"

Marley ignored him. "Charm the pants off people, that's what. My God, that man was putty in your hands. You're like a whole club of good ol' boys all on your own."

She produced a set of pills from the purse at her side and set them in front of him, then slid a glass of water beside them. "There ya go."

"Why do you think Austin always made me be the face of the company?"

Marley snorted, surely thinking of her antisocial boyfriend in a meeting like the one they'd just had. "That wouldn't have gone well."

Grant grunted as he swallowed the pills along with the whole glass of water. He'd slept like shit since that night in the club. And had trouble concentrating. He was actually pretty damn proud of himself for pulling off that meeting, even if he still had to wait to hear if they decided to advertise with *Gamers*.

Marley tentatively touched his arm. "You okay?"

He sighed. "Just tired. Lot on my mind."

"Anything I can do?"

He smiled at her. "Nah, I'll live."

She stood up and gathered her papers and purse. "I'm heading back to work then. Let me know if you need anything else."

"Thanks for sitting in on the meeting to make sure I didn't go off the rails."

Marley laughed. "Anytime."

He watched her leave and knew he should probably get out of the conference room and back to his office. But man, he needed a moment.

He'd prepared for this meeting in advance because big advertisers were a key to growing the magazine. And thank God he'd been prepared because this weekend had been a head trip. He couldn't forget the feel of Chloe's hands and skin and *fuck*, was he ever going to be able to think normally again?

And on top of his memories of what happened, he was anticipating what he hoped would happen next. He'd slipped Chloe his address and a date and time on a slip of paper, asking her to come to his house this weekend. He assumed she'd come in a role again, and he'd spend all week tossing and turning thinking about it.

He had never realized how much it turned him on to play games. Or maybe it was just because it was Chloe, but either way, he didn't want it to end anytime soon.

Of course, he needed to keep this from Ethan. Chloe clearly understood this was something they had to keep secret. Grant hated not telling his friend, especially in light of all he'd gone through, but this wasn't about Ethan. This was about Grant and Chloe and fulfilling each other's needs in some crazy way.

That couldn't be wrong, could it?

Grant stood up and stretched, his back cracking. He'd need to do some extra time on the treadmill this week so he could tire himself out. Maybe that was the only way he could sleep. Because he sure as hell wanted to be rested for whatever was in store for him this weekend.

Chapter Eight

The floor was clean, the tables dusted, and a candle currently burned, filling the house with the scent of—Grant checked the label—lilac blossoms. He sniffed. Kind of strong but it was better than smelling the soup he'd burned. He'd thrown the pot away to hide the evidence rather than let Sydney see what he'd done. She'd never stop chastising him.

Grant had even changed the sheets, even though he wasn't sure he and Chloe would actually make it into bed. He had fantasized all day about the couch and the kitchen table. He was too old to fuck on the stairs but the up against the wall in the hallway was a real possibility. Or maybe on the sink in the bathroom.

Damn, he was getting hard just thinking about it. He downed the rest of his wine and dropped his glass in the sink, wondering if Chloe would be on time. Sydney was sleeping over at a friend's house tonight, so Grant had the house to himself. He hoped Chloe came. It would suck if she stood him up, but he couldn't get enough of her. He thought about her all week to the point he was incredibly distracted at work. He felt a weird possessiveness over her, too, which was new for him. This was just sex, and only that. Hell, they didn't even call each other by their names. But was she doing this with other men? Was it just a fun game for her?

He pushed the thought aside. The hottest girl he'd ever been with wanted to sleep with him. Repeatedly. With role-playing kink. Why was he analyzing this shit?

His doorbell rang and he padded toward it in bare feet, the hem of his jeans brushing the floor. He rubbed his clammy hands on his pants. He rarely brought women here. And especially women he didn't even fuck as himself. Which was weird but oh so very hot.

He peered through the peephole. Chloe was standing on the front porch, large sunglasses over her eyes—even though it was nighttime—and wearing a belted trench coat.

When he opened the door, he gazed down to her bare legs and sky-high black heels.

"Mr. Osprey?" she asked, her lips a bright cherry red.

He leaned on the door and raised an eyebrow. "Yes."

Her pink tongue slipped out, wetting her bottom lip. "My handler said you have hired my services for the night. I only accept cash."

He nearly swallowed his tongue. So she wanted to play some *Pretty Woman* role, huh? He went from kinda hard to full mast.

"We agreed on two grand and I get you until two in the morning." He deliberately leered. "All of you. Every inch of you. However I want you. Suit you, Princess?"

The lapels of her trench coat quivered. "Suits me."

"Great." He stepped back and gestured inside. "Come in, please."

She brushed past him and he smelled strawberries. He shut and locked the door, then turned around to face Chloe.

She'd taken her sunglasses off and her hands were on her untied belt. In one practiced move, she flung open the edges of the coat and rolled her shoulders so the khaki material fluttered to the ground at her feet.

Grant had to shoot out a hand to brace himself on the wall because he suddenly had vertigo.

The physical parts of Chloe he loved the most were encased in lavender lace—a bra that didn't cover much, because he could see her hardened nipples poking through.

Her thong didn't cover much except for a small triangle scrap, hiding her pussy—which he knew she shaved bare—from his view.

Jesus, all that skin, that delicious lace, all for him.

She watched him with those green eyes, a sexy smirk to her mouth. She slowly twisted, so that her ankles were crossed, and showed him her back. She looked at him through her lashes over her shoulder. Only a string ran along the top of her ass and between her crease.

He was hard in his jeans, ridiculously so, and he hadn't even touched her yet. Hadn't yet taken that mouth or plunged his fingers in that tight heat. He was going to do all of that and then some.

He stepped toward her. "Hands on the wall. Ass out."

Her breath left her in a rush and she complied immediately, laying her hands—tipped with red nails—on the wall, then arched her back.

He raised a hand, bringing his palm down first on one

cheek, then the other, loving the sound of flesh smacking flesh, smiling at the pink skin he left behind.

She moaned and he reached for the string that covered her pussy, then tugged it aside roughly. He palmed her, sliding a middle finger between her folds.

As predicted, she was soaked already.

"Good girl," he murmured, pulling her thong off and tossing it to the floor. He gripped her hip and returned his hand to her wetness, plunging two fingers into her opening. She gasped, most likely surprised at how fast he was moving.

"Since I only get you until two in the morning, I'm going to make sure we get a couple of rounds in. First one is here. But this one's for me. Only me. Understand?"

Her cheek was pressed against the wall, eyes closed, hips surging as she bucked into his hand. He twisted his fingers. "Understand?"

She nodded, her mouth open, lips wet. With a grunt he flicked open the top button of his pants and pulled down his zipper, freeing his cock.

He pulled his hand away from her, giving her pussy a few smacks, wetting his palm with her fluids. Then he gripped his erection, coating himself with her arousal. The room smelled like sex and strawberries and he didn't have to stroke himself for long. He was so turned on by her ass in front of him, the dazed look on her face.

"I've been thinking about this, about marking you." The possessiveness he'd thought about earlier flared and he couldn't stop the claiming words rushing out of his mouth. "Push that ass toward me, sweetheart, I want to see it." He only had to roll his balls with his other hand and listen to the wet sounds of his hand stroking himself, and then he was coming, shooting all over her bare ass, watching as his release streaked her red skin white.

When he opened his eyes, she was watching him, her entire face flushed red. He let go of his sensitive cock and leaned his forehead against her back.

He ran his fingers over the come on her ass, rubbing it into her skin. "You look good with my come on you, Princess. Now get on your knees and clean me up."

• • •

Chloe was raw, an exposed, throbbing nerve as she pivoted and dropped to her knees on the hardwood floor.

Her muscles ached, and despite the cooling wetness on her back, her skin was on fire. What was it about Grant that made her feel naked? It had nothing to do with clothes, or exposed skin. It was his eyes that saw too much and his hands that tore away the film over her eyes.

It was him.

She tried to slip back into the working-girl role she swore she'd keep but as she leaned forward, lapping at the tip of Grant's still half-hard cock, it was through Chloe's eyes.

His hand rested on her hair, and she licked the vein on the underside of his shaft and nestled her face into the hair in his groin. When she pulled away, she pressed a kiss to his inner thigh. A kiss with Chloe's lips and Chloe's emotion.

As she sat back on her heels, breathing heavily, eyes staring blankly at Grant's bare feet, she thought about how she'd known this was a bad idea. Every encounter with Grant got more personal. He asked more and more of her, dismantling every roadblock she threw up. But she still had her role. So she clung to it and focused on the man who was fulfilling her fantasies.

A hand on her shoulder signaled her to stand, and she did on shaky legs. Grant stepped forward, forcing her to retreat until her back hit the wall behind her. Then he took her mouth with punishing force, shoving his tongue between her lips.

She pushed back, matching his passion with that of her own, as they dueled for the control of the kiss.

When he pulled back, his full lips were swollen and wet. "Fuck, you can kiss."

She smiled. "I like kissing you."

He laughed once and leaned in, sucking on her neck. She let her head fall back as his renewed erection pressed against her swollen flesh. She shifted her hips, trying to get closer, but Grant's head rose, and he pulled back. "Eager, huh?"

She made a frustrated sound in her throat and he grinned. He grabbed her wrist, pulling her behind him. "Bedroom."

She liked the sound of that.

When they reached his bed, he stood her at the end, deftly unclipped her bra and tossed it to the floor. He gently pushed on her shoulders, so she fell back onto the bed.

Fabric rustled and in seconds, he was on top of her, naked, his body flush with hers. He went right for her breasts, squeezing them, sucking on her nipples and manipulating her flesh until her nipples were aching and hard.

But still he continued, flicking the tip of his tongue on the stiff peaks, driving her out of her mind as she rocked her hips into him, wanting to be filled.

He finally let her go, giving each breast a soft smack. "I

think I could spend all day with these."

She arched her back and his eyes flared.

He reached to his nightstand, and she heard the crinkle of a wrapper.

Finally, finally she'd get him inside of her, where she'd been aching for him since she walked in the door.

A hand gripped her hip. "Close your eyes, Princess."

She did, even though she wasn't seeing much anyway, her body overwhelmed with the physical sensation of his body against hers.

Something soft touched her lips, rubbing across her flesh. It felt like smooth fabric and smelled clean, like laundry detergent. She opened her mouth and Grant pushed the fabric inside, just a small bit of it, enough for her to bite down.

When she opened her eyes, his eyes were on her lips. He lifted the end of the fabric that wasn't in her mouth and she recognized her panties, the ones Sari had left behind in the hotel room.

He gripped her chin, keeping her mouth closed. "These have tortured me for weeks, these panties you left behind. Now I get to torture you a little with them." His eyes were gleaming, his lips curled in a wicked smile. This was taking her out of the role a bit, and that was messing with her head. This wasn't lining up with her call girl routine. But Grant was hard, his cock pressing against her. This was turning him on, and she wasn't about to let him down after all he'd done for her. And she had to admit this was hot as hell, him fucking her while she was gagged with her own panties.

But damn Grant for not sticking to the plan.

She squeezed her eyes shut, and Grant's lips brushed over her eyelids, leaving a wet trail down her face, nuzzling under her ear.

His fingers plunged inside of her. "You want my cock here?"

His fingers, good Lord those fingers, they were twisting and curling and her body was surging into them, riding his hand. She could do this, she could play the role and block out anything that ruined it.

He took the panties out of her mouth and she opened her eyes. "I'm going to fuck you now, you understand?"

Yes, yes, that's exactly what she wanted. She wanted to be the call girl he fucked in his bed. The woman he used to get off. That's what she wanted and so she curled her hands around his biceps, her nails digging into his skin. "Fuck me," she said. "Get what you paid for."

He set his jaw and then plunged inside of her. He immediately began a punishing pace as he gripped her hips, watching their connection.

He was beautiful, his dirty-blond hair falling in his eyes, his blue irises blazing in the moonlight. Sweat shone off his shoulders, the tendons straining under his skin. "Fuck, Princess," he gasped. "Fuck, you always feel so good on my cock."

His cock felt good inside of her. "Am I worth two grand?"

He laughed roughly. "Don't tell your handler, but you could charge way more, Princess."

She gripped his shoulders tightly and lifted a leg, curling it around his thigh. "Yeah? I expect a hefty tip, then."

"I'd empty my bank account for you if you make it worth my while."

Well that was a challenge. She planted her right foot on the bed and with strength she didn't know she had, she flipped Grant onto his back.

His eyes widened as she straddled his hips and with one swift motion sank back down onto his cock.

She planted her hands onto his chest and swiveled her hips. She wanted to get as much out of this time as she could. She wasn't sure how long this could last, how long she could separate Chloe from the woman in Grant's fantasy. And she never wanted him to find out the difference.

So she worked her hips harder, ran her fingers up her sides, cupping her breasts, then into her hair.

Grant was staring at her breasts, which bounced with every jolt as she rode him hard.

She reached down, thumbing her clit, reaching for the orgasm that she knew was close, so close, as it always was with Grant.

"Fuck," he grunted, his fingers tightening on her thighs. "Fuck, fuck, I'm going to come, Chloe."

The veins in his neck were in sharp relief as he seemed to battle his climax, wanting to hold it off. She closed her eyes as her own orgasm curled her toes and forced a cry from her mouth.

Grant was right behind her, pulsing inside of her, his breath rasping from between his lips.

She propped herself up with one hand on his abs, rolling her hips slightly, clenching her inner muscles around his cock, cataloging the feel of him. And then she collapsed onto his chest as his arms wrapped around her back.

She wondered if he could ever like her as Chloe, if she could allow herself to let him in. But she couldn't imagine anything beyond failing him in some way or another. She wasn't this fantasy girl come to life. She was Chloe.

"Hey." Grant's voice was low as he shifted under her. "I

still owe you a tip."

Or not. Chloe sighed, the unfairness of the situation settling deep into her bones. This was her doing, after all. This role-playing. She'd set the parameters of their messed-up relationship. Of course he was only interested in playing the role. Grant was fun and carefree and so super-hot. He deserved a woman who wasn't a ridiculous, insecure mess like Chloe.

She took a deep breath and plastered on a smile as she rolled off him. He shifted to his side as she stood beside the bed, beginning to dress again.

"So," he said. "Two grand really set me back and I don't have much food in the house, but I know a place that makes a mean breakfast burrito. Open 24/7." He waggled his eyebrows. "What do you say?"

She froze. Was this an extension of their role-playing? Because she wasn't sure how much longer she had it in her to keep up the role. She was already exhausted and a little foggy from the sex and the facade she'd been keeping up since she got here. "Um…"

"I got a spare T-shirt or something you can wear, Chlo. Probably a pair of shorts or something, too." He shrugged, as if the shortened version of her name, said with affection, didn't steal her breath. "No one where we're going will care what you look like."

"No," she said, firmly and quickly. The last thing she wanted to do right now was go out in public, as Chloe, without the armor of her clothes or her role. It was no big deal to Grant—Ethan had said he was social, had friends all over town—but that wasn't her. Going out now would take energy she just didn't have. And the thought of making small talk while still feeling the effects of him inside of her didn't sound appealing at all.

Grant was checking his phone. "What?" he asked distractedly. "If you don't like burritos, we can just go somewhere else—"

"No," she said again and this time he looked up, brow furrowed.

"No what?"

"No, I can't go out."

He put his phone to the side and sat up, watching her closely now. "You can't go out tonight or you...can't go out ever? What exactly are you telling me here, Chloe?"

Chloe wasn't made for relationships. She didn't know to communicate effectively. She couldn't even do it with her own family, couldn't help them through their grief or knit them all back together.

Emotions and relationships were hard and too gray. She'd stick with debugging computers and out of relationships she had no business being in.

And above all, she'd stick to the roles she played.

She lifted her chin. "What, you think you're my only client tonight?"

He blinked at her, clearly confused. "Uh..."

She needed to get out of here before she lost her mind. "So I'm sorry, but you'll have to do your midnight burrito run by yourself. If you want my services again, you have my handler's number?"

He was still staring at her like she'd gone crazy. Something flitted over his face. Frustration, maybe? A little bit of anger? "Uh," he mumbled again. "Yeah. Yeah sure."

She was letting him down already; that was what Chloe

did. So this was time for her to get the hell out while maybe he still had the desire to see her again. In a role, of course.

God, how was this her life?

She paused in the doorway, biting her lip, thinking she should just go, just leave, but Grant deserved something. She turned her head, to look at him as he sat in his bed, brow furrowed. "Sorry but it's better this way. What we do now. You wouldn't want the real me."

He looked even more confused. "What does that mean, the real you?"

That was all she had in her. "You wouldn't understand."

She raised her hand and blew him a flirty kiss, even though she felt anything but flirty, then dashed downstairs, pulling on her crumpled trench coat as she wrenched open the door, getting the hell out as fast as she could, leaving behind a confused Grant sitting naked in his bed.

But she couldn't imagine anything beyond failing him in some way or another. She wasn't this fantasy girl come to life. She was Chloe.

And Chloe would never be enough for a man like Grant.

Chapter Nine

What the hell was that?

Grant stared at his bedroom door, blinking. Seriously, what the hell?

He'd gone from having an amazing orgasm to wanting some damn burritos to Chloe disappearing on him before he could figure out what the hell had happened.

He hadn't even really thought too much about it, asking her out to get a bite to eat with him. It'd just felt…right. That had been some amazing sex and all he wanted to do was eat and stare into Chloe's eyes.

Was that wrong? And why the hell had she looked at him like he'd just asked her to make some lifelong commitment? It was just burritos for fuck's sake.

You wouldn't want the real me. What did that even mean? Chloe had a lot of sides to her, he saw now. Why couldn't he want more than one?

Grant ran a hand through his hair and tugged, wishing

Chloe was back in his bed, because he wasn't hungry anymore.

After he'd slept with her the first time, he'd been mostly glad he didn't have to deal with the complication of a committed relationship in his life. He was committed to Sydney and his friends and that was all he had time for. That was all he wanted.

He couldn't want more with Chloe, could he? The idea of wanting to spend more time with her after sex had sounded damn good. But nah, this was probably better, right? No strings. She hadn't wanted him and so he could live with that. His ego was still intact.

Except, his stomach hurt. It seemed like the roles were all that Chloe planned to give him. And for the first time since they started this charade, he thought that maybe it wasn't enough.

The next morning, Grant sipped his coffee and watched as Sydney stuffed her mythology textbook she'd been studying at breakfast into her book bag.

He'd slept like shit last night because his whole house smelled like stupid flowers from the candle and strawberries from Chloe's hair and fuck it all, he wanted to rip his nose off his face.

To top it off, he missed his daughter. They'd both been so busy lately, he hadn't had a chance to sit down and talk to her like he usually did. He felt like a crappy parent. He needed to get his head out of the clouds and focus on his daughter. "Hey, we never got talk about career day. Did you like the professional you spoke to?"

Sydney brushed her hair over her shoulder and glanced at the clock. "It was awesome, I had the best mentor."

"Really?" He had been pleased with her school. He imagined it was a lot of work to ask community professionals to take time to talk to students, but it was invaluable in his opinion.

"Yeah, she was really nice and we got along really well. I learned a lot about the field and she made me super-excited about it."

"That's great. What does she do?"

Sydney dug in her book bag. "She finds problems in software and fixes it." She pulled out a business card and handed it to him. "And I told her I'd like to meet up sometime to talk more. She said sure but that she'd want a parent present. I guess so she didn't get in trouble."

Grant couldn't speak, because his tongue froze to the roof of his mouth as he stared at the business card of one Chloe Talley.

He'd never in a million years thought she'd be at the career fair, so that must have been Ethan's doing.

He looked up at his daughter. "Chloe Talley?"

"Yeah, do you know her?"

"Sweetheart, Talley is Ethan's last name."

Sydney frowned. "But he's not married."

"No, he's not. This is his sister."

"Really?"

"Yes, really. Did she say anything about your last name?"

Sydney pursed her lips. "I'm not sure I ever said my last name. I told her I was Sydney."

The coincidence really wasn't that great. The community

wasn't that big and the school was surely eager to get a female member of the STEM field.

"Something wrong?" Sydney asked.

"No, no, just…you know, this is cool." God, that sounded lame to his own ears.

"Well, when I email her, I'll tell her — "

"No," he said before he could think about it. "No, uh, we'll just have it be a surprise when she agrees to meet, okay?" God, he was a deceitful prick, and he was using his daughter to see the woman he wanted to sleep with again. But Chloe had said he wouldn't want the *real* her, and now he was determined to find out who the hell that was.

Sydney shrugged. "Okay, well I gotta catch my bus. Later, Dad!"

He waved halfheartedly, and maybe mumbled a good-bye. He clutched Chloe's business card, running his fingers over the lettering. There was no phone number. Just an email address. He filed it away in his wallet.

By the afternoon Grant had a headache. A giant one. But he was pretty sure he had reached the daily limit of ibu-profen about three pills ago, so he didn't think he should take any more. Especially because he was supposed to be working.

His office door at *Gamers* opened and shut, and then the leather of the chair in front of his desk squeaked. He raised his head.

Austin sat across from him, his elbow propped up on the armrest, his chin in his hand. He stared at Grant with raised eyebrows.

"What?" Grant said irritably.

"You tell me."

Austin was slightly smug. Grant didn't like it. "What are you doing here?"

Austin gestured toward the door. "Marley was concerned. She said you've been holed up here all day and didn't flirt once with the hot-ass mail carrier."

Grant frowned. "I don't flirt with her."

"Yes you do. And she said you got the Erotech advertising account—congrats on that—but that you didn't do that little jig thing you usually do when you land big accounts."

"It's called a Riverdance," Grant mumbled.

Austin ignored him. "So what's going on?"

Grant harrumphed and crossed his arms over his chest, leaning back in his chair. "Since when do you pop in to my office to talk about my feelings?"

Austin didn't hesitate. "Since Marley's in my bed and she told me to get in here."

Grant squinted his eyes. "So this is under duress."

Austin tilted his head. "Somewhat. But I do care why you're acting like a hermit."

Grant ran his finger along the edge of a yellow notepad, just so he didn't have to look at Austin. He could email Chloe. He had her email address but somehow that seemed very lame in light of what they had done. And what would he even *say* in the email?

"It's a woman," he blurted out to Austin.

Silence. Grant slowly lifted his gaze. His best friend stared at him with a passive face.

Grant scowled. "No response?"

"You said three words. I'm going to need more so I know how to react properly."

Sometimes Grant wanted to punch Austin. "I met a

woman and she's under my skin, but she doesn't want me. At least I don't think she wants me."

Austin's face changed now, softening slightly. He leaned forward. "And you want more?"

"I guess I'd like the chance to get to know her better. It's complicated but she isn't comfortable being herself around me."

"And you can't convince her?"

Grant threw up his hands. "I have no idea. But Austin, man, she's beautiful and smart as hell. In bed, she's…" Grant stared out the window of his office, picturing Chloe's long hair draped down her back in the hotel room in Philadelphia, then her breasts bared to him in the supply closet of the club, and the sight of her braced against the wall in his house, ass pushed out for him. Just him. "In bed, she's out of this world," he finished, thinking that phrase didn't even come close to what Chloe was like when she let herself go.

Austin sighed. "You're a persuasive guy. You can't give up this easily. Imagine if I would have given up on Marley."

Grant wasn't so sure it was in his power to talk to Chloe. And even though the thought made him want to hurl, maybe Ethan was his only hope in this whole mess. Grant wished he could just forget about her, and return to his uncomplicated life but he simply couldn't. He'd seen glimpses of the Chloe she seemed intent on hiding—the loving sister, the smart businesswoman, the caring mentor. He wanted her to let him in.

Grant tapped his fingers on his desk. "You're right. Maybe I'll get in touch with her."

Austin stood up and stuck his hands in his pockets. "I'm taking Marley out to lunch. Do you need anything?"

Grant shook his head. "No, and thanks for coming in to talk to me. Tell Marley I appreciate it."

"I hope I helped."

"Yeah, you did. Thanks, buddy."

When Austin had closed the office door behind him, Grant stared at the phone on his desk. Talking to Ethan, coming clean, would be one of the hardest things he'd ever have to do. Ethan was a rational man, but not when it came to his sisters. He carried guilt on his shoulders like a crippling weight.

Grant wondered how much Chloe was affected by Samantha's death.

He wondered if it had anything to do with how she was reacting to him.

Before he chickened out, he picked up the phone and dialed Ethan.

"Yes," his friend answered.

"Hey, it's Grant."

"I know that." Ethan sounded irritated and out of breath.

"What's going on? Are you okay?"

Ethan blew out a breath into the phone. "I'm fine, it's… Chloe."

Grant leaned forward, gripping the edge of his desk with white knuckles. "What's wrong? Is she okay?"

"I've been calling her and she isn't answering. She texted that she was fine and to stop bugging her. But *fine* means *not fine*, right? I know it's been a while, but I'm pretty sure when a woman says she's fine, it's time to panic."

That seemed a little nosy to Grant, but then, he didn't know their relationship. Still, his chest squeezed. Now definitely wasn't the time to come clean about what he and

Chloe had been doing. He hoped Chloe was okay, and vaguely wondered if this was his fault, if he'd pushed her too far, made her feel unsafe in any way.

Shit.

"Is this about Samantha—"

"No," Ethan said quickly.

Grant didn't ask and he hoped Ethan knew what he was talking about. He did still wonder if Chloe had come to terms with her sister's passing. Grant wanted to be able to be there for Chloe, to tell Ethan that he cared for her and wanted to help. He hated that he was in this helpless position. "If there's anything I can do—"

"It's fine, Grant, but I have to go. If she doesn't pick up my phone calls, I'm going over to see her. Did you need something?"

"Uh, well." He licked his lips. "I was actually going to ask you for Chloe's phone number."

Silence.

Grant never could stay quiet during silence. "I had some questions…for a friend…about…security." He was fumbling over his words. No way would Ethan not see right through that. "But it can wait. Take care of your sister, Ethan."

There was a pause. "Will do."

The call ended.

Grant stared at the phone for a minute, silent in its receiver. Then he pulled up his Internet browser and began to research grief. It made him feel a little bit less helpless.

• • •

Chloe lay in bed staring at the ceiling.

She couldn't even get herself off properly anymore.

After the fuckup that was the night at Grant's, Chloe had holed herself up in her apartment. Ethan had been calling her all day and night. She'd blown him off with an "I'm fine" text, but who knew how long that would hold him off. Like a true introvert, she needed plenty of alone time to recharge before she had to talk to anyone again. The night at Grant's had been more than she could handle. She'd come so close, so close to letting him in but she wasn't ready for that.

Not when her family was still a mess and Ethan still needed watching. Even if he denied it. No, this was fine. This was okay.

If only she could have a freaking orgasm. She decided on her go-to fantasy, which was Kahl Drogo in Game of Thrones. So she was Daenerys predragon but whatever. That Daenerys was still pretty badass.

She lay on her back while morning sun crept across the floor of her bedroom and slipped her fingers into her panties.

She imagined big Kahl Drogo with his long, dark braid and his kohl-rimmed eyes grabbing her thighs and plunging into her again, and again and...

Blue eyes flashed in her vision.

Wait, what? Kahl Drogo didn't have blue eyes. He had brown eyes.

And he didn't smile, and call her Princess. She was Kahleesi, dammit. Kahleesi.

Come for me, Princess.

No, shit, that wasn't Kahl's guttural tone, that was Grant's deep, friendly one.

This always worked, her fantasies. This was her escape,

her way to get away and now all she could hear was Grant's voice and all she could see were his blue eyes, his clenched jaw.

Her hips were moving on their own accord and her fingers were slipping through the wetness over her clit.

She was going to come. She was going to come with the phantom Grant on top of her, inside of her, whispering her name and demanding things of her she didn't want to give.

The orgasm rocketed through her and when she opened her mouth, she didn't praise Kahl for the excellent fucking. No, when she came it was with Grant's name whispered on her lips.

And then she lay there, her fingers wet, her body exhausted, dread gnawing at her belly.

She was so much deeper into Grant that she had thought. He'd broken her with his skilled hands. His dirty words. The way he burned her with his blazing blue eyes.

You'll never be what he needs, a voice in her head said.

She took a minute to gather her bearings, then got out of bed to start her day.

Half an hour later, while she was eating breakfast, there was a knock on her door. She stuck her finger in her mouth, catching the stray drop of syrup that she'd caught off her plate.

When she opened the door, Ethan stood there, hands in the pockets of his track pants, long-sleeved shirt stretched across his broad chest. "What's going on?"

"Why aren't you answering my calls?"

She feigned ignorance. "What do you mean? I texted you."

Ethan stared at her, not buying it.

She sighed. "I was busy."

Ethan stepped inside, forcing her to take a step back so he could come in. He shut the door behind him and looked around her place. "Working?"

Not really. "Yes."

He frowned and then sniffed, his expression softening. "Pancakes?"

She rolled her eyes and walked into the kitchen, listening to Ethan's steps behind her. "Did you come over on the false pretense of worrying about me just to get some breakfast?"

He'd done that when she was on a Game of Thrones food kick. She'd bought a cookbook and made all kinds of treats from the books, like lemon cakes and Pentoshi duck. She even blogged about it, which Ethan said was the nerdiest thing she'd ever done.

Whatever. Sansa was right; those lemon cakes were delicious.

But she liked making Ethan happy, so she fed him pancakes and listened to him talk about work and afterward, they sat on the couch to watch morning news shows.

He'd done this when they were kids, hang out with her like this. She'd read him books and he'd laugh at her voices, while Samantha lay on the bed, tossing a ball in the air.

Chloe wanted to share that memory with Ethan. She wanted to talk to him about Samantha, but when she tried in the past, his entire body would stiffen. He'd retreat into his shell and that made Chloe's heart hurt even worse. She hadn't just lost Samantha that day. She'd lost Ethan, too, or at least the Ethan he'd been. The loving, affectionate brother. The one who smiled a lot and laughed. He had the best laugh.

And she'd also lost her family, that cohesive unit that had been her foundation.

She wished she could confess all of this to Ethan, but she didn't want to add to the guilt he'd already placed on himself. Samantha would have been able to do it. If it were Chloe who died, Samantha would have kept the family together. She wouldn't have let Ethan fall so deep within himself that he'd become a different person.

And she wouldn't turn down Grant Osprey, the man of Chloe's dreams. The thought of Grant's smile, his laugh, his teasing humor and oh God, his hands, made her ache and burn all at the same time.

She fell asleep on the couch and woke up to the smell of something burning. Rubbing her eyes, she sat up and peered over the couch. Ethan was frowning at the toaster oven, and it made her smile to see him crouch and peer inside.

She stood up, clutching the blanket around her shoulders, and walked into the kitchen.

Ethan looked up when he heard her footsteps, still frowning. "I tried to make you toast for lunch. I think it's burnt."

She looked into the toaster oven at the blackened bread. "Yep, looks pretty burnt."

He huffed and pointed to a pan on the stovetop. "Well, I didn't burn the soup. It's just a can so the sodium content might kill you, but at least it's food."

So she sat at the table and let Ethan serve her some soup. She stirred it absentmindedly, thinking of what she'd done that morning, who she'd been thinking about.

"Chloe?" Ethan asked as he washed the soup pan.

"Yeah?"

He paused for a minute, then shut off the water and dried his hands. "Are you seeing anyone?"

She blinked at the sudden question, and stammered out the first thing her panicked mind thought of. "N-no."

Ethan chewed on his lip. "No?"

That wasn't really a lie. She wasn't sure what she and Grant had done—were still doing?—had any sort of classification. She shook her head.

Ethan dropped the towel on the counter. "Okay, just wondering. Uh, Grant asked me for your number. Something about a security question. You know anything about that?"

Her blood roared in her ears. Grant had to be slightly desperate if he was willing to stick his neck out and ask Ethan. Again, she could do nothing but shake her head.

Ethan shrugged. "I didn't give it to him. Do you mind if I do?"

Her mind whirled. "Uh, I'm busy. With work…and stuff."

Ethan waved her off, as if he was relieved about it all. "I'll blow him off. No worries."

She breathed out a sigh of relief, even as a pang of regret hit her in the chest.

While Ethan finished cleaning up, Chloe made her way into her office to check her email.

She scanned through them, getting rid of spam. An unfamiliar email caught her eye—SydKid247. She clicked on it and read the email from Sydney, asking if they could meet for coffee within the next couple of days to discuss more about Chloe's job.

Her first inclination was to say no, no way. For a few minutes when they were chatting at the career fair, Chloe thought she could maybe make a difference in the girl's life. But Sydney was so vibrant. So excited about the future ahead of her. What could Chloe do for her? Nothing, that was what. She'd inevitably let Sydney down, maybe even give her a negative opinion of women in her profession, and she didn't think she could live with herself if that happened. But the girl's email was so excitable, full of exclamation points about how she wanted to see Chloe again…about how her dad said it was okay, and that he'd come to supervise, like Chloe had asked.

Chloe set her jaw, deciding then and there she would *not* fail this kid. She was going to do her damnedest to help her. Hell, she had to start somewhere. Before she changed her mind, she wrote back saying yes, she'd love to meet up.

And like the last time she'd seen Sydney, she'd be comfortable enough to be herself.

Chapter Ten

Chloe walked toward the front of the coffee shop, feeling a little exposed, but psyched by the opportunity to do something *positive*. She'd agreed to meet Sydney on Friday after school, and Chloe had been looking forward to it all week. The teenager was fun and excited and she reminded Chloe of all the reasons she loved her job. Why Chloe herself had value in the world. It was…refreshing.

It also helped ease the ache of disappointing Grant. That wound was still too fresh for Chloe to do anything but wait for it to heal over.

But she couldn't think about that now. She took a deep breath and donned her professional Chloe hat, pushed open the door, and glanced around the coffee shop. It wasn't too busy, but there was a decent crowd. Sydney, her blond hair pulled back into a ponytail, waved at her from a table. A man sat across from her, his back to her. Chloe figured this was Sydney's father. She walked toward their table, bringing her hand out to shake his. He stood when Sydney waved, then turned slowly.

His head was down, and when he lifted it, Chloe's steps faltered.

Grant stood there, his blue eyes cautious, completely unsurprised to see her. Chloe's eyes darted to Sydney. "Hi, Miss Talley. This is my dad, Grant Osprey." Sydney studied her face and frowned. "He said he knows you? I didn't know you were Ethan's sister."

Dad.

Grant had a daughter.

And not just any daughter, but Sydney.

Chloe hadn't known he had a child, or maybe she had at one time, but had forgotten. Either way, her mind spun.

She'd planned to avoid him as much as possible, make excuses whenever Ethan mentioned his presence, hoping time would begin to smooth over the hurt of not being able to have Grant.

This...this was too soon. She was too fragile, still too raw from their last night together. Yet here he was, his hand out-stretched, his eyes pleading with her to stay. This couldn't be happening again, this freaking repeat of the dinner with Ethan.

Chloe glanced at Sydney, who was watching them curiously now, a little furrow between her brows. If it wasn't for her, Chloe would have turned around and walked back out, just put this all behind her. But she couldn't do that to the girl who'd sent her an excited email with emoticons.

So she stuck out her hand, feeling the trembles up her arm. "Hi, Grant, nice to see you again." She turned to Sydney. "Yes, I'm Ethan's sister. I...guess I never got your last name so I didn't put it all together."

"I should have noticed your last name but I was nervous and—"

Chloe waved her hand, taking a seat, ever aware of Grant's eyes on her as he sat, too. "No worries, Sydney. Anyway, I'm so glad you asked me to coffee."

Sydney smiled. "Dad can get you a drink."

"Oh, that's—"

"What would you like, Chloe?" Grant leaned close, closer than he probably should have.

Chloe sucked in a breath. "Um, just a latte is fine."

"Coming right up."

He stood, the scent of his cologne and skin right under her nose. She wanted to nuzzle into him, feel his heat, but in one step he was gone, walking toward the counter.

His absence gave her time to collect herself, which she desperately needed if she was going to be any help to Sydney. That's why she was here, for this bright teenager who sat across from her with a brilliant smile and blue eyes. Which she now saw was Grant, all Grant. She was a beautiful girl.

"Thank you so much for coming, Miss Talley. I had some more questions, if that's all right." Sydney dug a spiral-bound notebook out her book bag and sat it on the table in front of her. Then she flipped open the cover and smoothed down a sheet covered in pen. She looked uncertain as she bit her lip and lifted her gaze to Chloe. "Is this okay?"

Chloe went for her best smile. "Of course! Just a bit nervous that I won't be of any help to you, or that I'll embarrass myself in front of your father." That was pure honesty.

Sydney beamed. "Oh, well just picture Dad and I in our pj's! That's what you told me, remember? I'll wear unicorns and Dad will wear…um…football ones or something."

That wasn't helping, not at all, because now all Chloe could think about was Grant in bed, not wearing pj's, oh no, he was wearing nothing at all. And she was slipping into the sheets with him, leaning in to kiss those full lips as his hand cupped her ass —

A steaming latte was placed on the table in front of her, then Grant sat down, a fresh cup in his hand. He took a sip, raising his eyebrows over the rim at her.

She wanted to take this latte and pour it on his pants. He'd shown up here, knowing he'd be seeing her. Sydney must have shown him her business card. While Chloe had been completely in the dark. It wasn't fair.

But she'd rally. Of course she would. Because Sydney thought she was important and dammit, Chloe could at least pretend to be for the next forty-five minutes or so.

And as Sydney began her questions — about when Chloe first became interested in programming, what classes she took in high school, and where she went to college — Chloe lost herself in talking about her work. She didn't like talking about herself, but this came naturally to her, and it was for Sydney's benefit. The teenager scribbled notes as Chloe talked, Sydney's little tongue touching the corner of her mouth as she concentrated. Every once in a while, Grant would shift his weight, but he kept silent and in time, Chloe relaxed. In a way, the two of them knew her in ways many people didn't. Although Chloe was highly sought-after in her field, the attention Sydney was giving her made her feel better than any award, any paycheck, any clap on the back.

Sydney talked, too, about her dreams and goals. They talked about baking and cooking, and Sydney promised to send a recipe for shortbread she was working on, and Chloe was going to send one for chicken fajitas in return. Grant perked up at that, which made Chloe forget herself for a minute and smile at him, picturing him enjoying a meal she cooked. He returned her smile easily, happily, and she had to look away.

And then their time was up. Sydney gathered her book bag and kissed her father on the cheek, then hugged Chloe, and before Chloe realized what she was going on, the girl was out the door of the coffee shop. On the sidewalk in front, she greeted another girl, and the two walked off together.

"She's meeting a friend to go shopping at the nearby strip mall. Sarah's mom is taking them home." Grant's voice was behind her, and she turned to look at him.

Chloe sipped her latte and thought about what to say. She should get up and leave, but her legs were trembling. She wasn't sure she could walk without making a fool of herself. "So you knew I'd be here."

"I did."

Chloe met his gaze.

He sighed and leaned forward. "I was worried you'd refuse to come, and Sydney would have been crushed."

Chloe narrowed her eyes. "I would never have stood up Sydney because of you. That girl is the sweetest teenager I think I've ever met. I would have braved a blizzard to get here for her." The vehemence in her voice surprised her, and it surprised Grant, too, if his widened eyes were any indication. She cleared her throat. "I didn't know you had a daughter."

Grant cocked his head. "Ethan never mentioned it?"

Chloe shrugged. "Maybe at one time he had, but I didn't

remember. You didn't mention it either."

Grant's jaw ticked. "You set a lot of ground rules about what we were allowed to talk about."

She looked away. Because he had a point.

"Chloe—"

"I should go."

"Dammit." His voice was a harsh whisper. "I've thought of nothing but you for a week. Ethan told me you weren't answering his calls and I was worried. And then you show up here, looking more beautiful than I've ever seen you, and you spent an hour of your time making my daughter's entire year. So if you can sit there and tell me that I mean nothing to you except for what we did physically, then tell me. And I'll leave you alone."

The tears were threatening and no way would she cry in a coffee shop. "I think you know perfectly well that I can't say that."

He leaned closer, his hand on her thigh, his face tilted into hers. "Then why won't you give us a try? Let's start over. I'll take you out on a date, and I'll treat you like a princess. We'll come clean to Ethan and hopefully he won't rip my nuts off."

She looked at him through her lashes. "You don't understand," she whispered, the knot in her throat threatening to choke her.

"Then make me understand," he pleaded. "Give me that much, Chloe."

"That's just it." He had to see. Why couldn't he see? "You don't want Chloe."

His face darkened. "You can't tell me that I don't want you."

"You don't know me." Her voice was pleading.

He cocked his head. "No? I know you're smart, one of the best at what you do. When you talk about your job, your whole face lights up. You cook like a fucking dream. I stole a whole container of that soup you made out of Ethan's refrigerator." He leaned closer, so his lips were right at her ear. "I know you get wet at the sound of my voice, that you love my tongue, that you crave how I fuck you. I know you think I'm funny even when you try to act like I'm not. And that's all you, Chloe, that's not whatever act you think you're putting on. I see right through all that bullshit. And despite this conversation, I like what I see."

She shook her head, desperate to get out of here, desperate to end this conversation, but Grant wasn't done. He cupped her cheek, rubbing gently with his thumb as he met her eyes. "As much as I love fucking you any way I can get you, I want the chance to make love to Chloe. Think about how good that would be, sweetheart. I'd take my time, licking you, working your clit with my tongue. There'd be no rush. Just you and me. And then I'd wrap your legs around my hips and I'd enter that wet pussy slowly, so fucking slowly, it'd be torture for both of us."

This was torture right now. His words. Because how badly did she want that? She imagined cooking with Grant, wearing nothing but his shirt. He'd walk up behind her, place his hand on her ass possessively while she let him sample the sauce from the tip of her spoon. He'd say, "That's delicious, sweetheart," in that smooth voice of his. They'd dine by candlelight and then later that night, in bed, she'd straddle him and ride him until they both passed out in exhaustion.

But that was dream Chloe. The one who had her life

together, who knew how to have meaningful, honest relationships. A dream Chloe who didn't fail her family to the point it completely fractured.

Grant was still talking. "It'd be so good, Chloe."

"You don't know that," she whispered.

"And you're not giving me chance to prove it to you. You're not giving *us* a chance. And this surprises the hell out of me, but I want to go grocery shopping and argue over whether to buy Heinz or generic ketchup. I want to drive in a car with you and see if that cute mouth swears at other drivers. I want to go to a baseball game with you and sing 'Take Me Out to the Ballgame.' I want the chance to get to know you better. But you're not going to let me get that chance, are you?"

She couldn't take the leap. She couldn't. Her throat grew tight, and her chest constricted. All those things sounded amazing in theory, but she didn't think she could live up to any of that. She let people down, wasn't who they expected or needed her to be. She didn't want to give Grant hope and then let him down, too. "I can't."

"Why?" he demanded.

She took a deep breath "I'm not a princess. Or a dirty maid. Or a call girl. I'm not any of those things. I'm Chloe Talley and I'm a mess. I read romance novels and I wear really ugly gaucho pants in my apartment and I usually have stained shirts from cooking." Her lip was trembling. She could feel it now. "And I'm not strong. I'm not strong at all. In fact, I let people down. I'm not charming like you and I don't like social places unless I can wear a costume and pretend to be someone else. The reason is because I don't like what I see. I don't like Chloe. And everything was fine until you made me want to give you more. And I can't give you that."

She brushed the back of her hand across her eyes as Grant's face went slack.

"So just give up. Please." Her voice cracked, but she soldiered on. "If you care about me, you'll give this up."

She grabbed her purse off the table and stood up, looking down at Grant who stared up at her with a stricken face. "And thanks for the latte."

Then she walked out, leaving Grant behind. And she hoped, for both of their sakes, this would be the last time he'd have to watch her leave.

• • •

Chloe could have slapped him across the face and it would have stung less than her words.

A weight was sitting on his chest, and the coffee that had been delicious five minutes ago now tasted bitter in his mouth.

He stared at his hands clasped between his knees. He should get up, throw his cup in the trash, and drive home. He should heed Chloe's wishes. But that small glimpse of the inner-workings of Chloe's mind had only succeeded in making him fall deeper.

Plus, he'd never been good at following rules.

Games had always been part of Grant's sex life. Role-playing was welcomed and encouraged. With Chloe, it'd been amazing at first, but that last time at his house, he'd grown tired of the act. He wanted to look her in the eye— Chloe, not whatever role she'd taken on for the day—and hear her say his name.

He wanted to wake up in bed with her in the morning, roll over and see her smiling at him with a fresh face and bed head. He wanted to curl up with her under a blanket and watch reality TV on his couch. Totally different than his normal date—wining and dining—but Chloe brought out his inner cuddler.

Had he ever wanted that before? Well, no. But then other women weren't Chloe. He'd been shocked right away at their unprecedented chemistry and then he started to see the real Chloe, the shy girl beneath the clothes, the chef, the loving sister. The woman who was determined to be a role model for his daughter.

The problem was that although he had an agenda to actually talk to Chloe each time they met, she scrambled his brains with her mouth and her ass and her ridiculously perfect tits.

Damn her.

Her determination not to let Sydney down was probably what did him in. His daughter's own mother didn't have a desire to stick around, but Chloe had been adamant that she would be there for Sydney. For his baby girl.

He stood up, threw his coffee cup away, and jogged out of the door. He turned the corner of the coffee shop and kept going down the alley on the way to the parking lot.

He caught a glimpse of Chloe's back ahead of him as she disappeared behind the building. He ran harder, and his shoes pounded the pavement as he rounded the corner. Chloe was there, walking toward her car. She didn't have a chance to look up before he grabbed her arm, spinning her around and backing her up against the brick wall of the coffee shop.

"Chloe," he said, crowding her with his body. Her eyes were huge, tear tracks on her cheeks. He cupped her face, brushing away the wetness with his thumb. "I do care, and that's exactly why I can't let you walk away from me. Not after dropping that on me."

"Please—"

He shook his head. "Tell me what's going on. Maybe I can help or—"

"No, I can handle it, I—"

"Chloe, I hate to break it to you, but no. I don't think you can handle whatever this is because, frankly, you don't seem to be doing such a good job at it."

She scowled a little at him, and he liked it, that he'd sparked some fire in her to override her sadness.

"What did you mean when you said you let people down?"

She nibbled on her bottom lip, gaze locked on his. Her eyes skittered away, resting on a spot over his shoulder, before they came back to his face. "It should have been me."

He furrowed his brow. "What should have been you?"

"In the car with Ethan. Instead of Samantha. Samantha was the one everyone loved. She was charming and beautiful. She had lots of friends. She would have been an amazing mother."

"Chloe, don't say that—"

"If it had been me who died, Samantha would have been able to keep the family together. She was strong like that. She would have been able to help my parents through their grief and she would have been able to prevent Ethan from turning into a depressed recluse." Her voice lowered to a whisper. "She would have been able to handle all of this. And I can't. Chloe can't. And I know it's creepy to talk about myself in the third person, but I'm doing it anyway."

He smiled a little at that. Her heart was huge, his Chloe. He'd seen it firsthand in the way she dealt with her brother and in the way she befriended his daughter. But there wasn't room for him, he now saw. Which made him want to put his fist through the wall beside her head.

Most of all, though, he saw she was trying to fit everyone else's problems inside, trying to take them all on her shoulders. He knew Ethan was estranged from his parents, but that wasn't her fault. And for her to think it was on her shoulders to bring them together wasn't fair to her.

"Have you talked to Ethan about this?" he asked.

She shook her head. "He doesn't like to talk about Samantha, or our parents."

"Yeah? And you think that's fair to you?" He hated this, that she'd carried this around for years. "You're not responsible for how your family is dealing with the loss of your sister. It was horrible and unfortunate, but you can't place all of this on your head."

"But Samantha was the glue of our family and I was just…an extra. She was necessary and it's never been more apparent since she died that I'm not necessary."

She didn't think she was necessary. His heart was breaking open right there. "Don't think for one minute that everyone wouldn't have been just as devastated if you were the one who died. Your family loves you. Your brother adores you."

"Because I'm the only sister left—"

"That's not true and I think you know it."

Chloe was cracking; he could see little bits of clarity peeking through the pinholes of her sadness. So he kept talking. "You can't take all this responsibility on your shoulders. Have you even taken time to grieve her? Or have you been focused on everyone else?"

She didn't answer, but the holes were getting larger. He was making progress.

"If your family knew what you were putting yourself through, they'd be devastated. I know they would. Ethan would never ever want you to feel like this. So for their sakes, for your own sake, please realize this, Chloe."

"I don't know what to do to fix this," she whispered.

"Chloe," he whispered. "I think the first step is realize that you *can't* fix this. And that's not your fault."

She sniffed.

"Talk to your family," he said. "And then set yourself up with a grief counselor. Have you talked to anyone about this?"

She shook her head.

"I can look some up for you. And I'd go with you, too, if you wanted. Will you let me do that?" If he couldn't be her lover, he'd be her friend.

Her lips wobbled. The cracks weren't getting any bigger. Her attention was wavering now and he could see her retreat into herself. "Chloe—"

"I can't do this," she whispered. "It's too much and my life is still so scattered and…"

The extreme high he'd been riding crashed down into the ground.

"But—"

She shook her head and slid out from between him and

the wall. He let her go, even though he didn't want to, even though it felt unnatural. He'd said his piece; he'd pleaded. He thought he'd gotten to her but apparently not.

She swallowed and placed her hand over his. ' You're a good man, Grant Osprey."

His smile felt brittle. "I'd love to get the chance to show you just how good I can be."

But she wasn't giving him that chance, because with a sad, sad smile, she turned and walked away. And Grant wasn't sure how long he stood there in the parking lot, wondering where he was going to go from here. All he knew was that he wasn't quite ready to give up yet. And he was pretty sure where he needed to head to next.

Chapter Eleven

Chloe stared at the suitcase on her bed. She could still feel Grant's hand in hers. She could still hear his voice in her ear, telling her that he'd be there for her.

Her. Chloe Talley.

It had taken all of her strength not to hand over her heart to him right then and there. And that would have been wrong. Now that she was home and had a moment to think, she realized that had been her problem all along—she'd been handing her heart out to everyone else. To her parents, to Ethan, to the memory of her sister. She'd never kept a part for herself and certainly didn't keep a part to share with the love of her life.

Before she could figure out if she was capable of that with Grant, she had some things to do. She hadn't wanted to make him any promises, in case she never got to that place she thought she could give him her heart.

But if she did make it there, she hoped he was still willing to put up with her. She had to try. Not just for Grant, but for herself, too.

So she was packing to visit her parents. She'd called and told them and although surprised, they sounded happy to see her.

She'd also called Ethan and the man was prompt so any minute now…

There was a knock at the door.

She left her half-packed suitcase on her bed and walked to her front door. Through the peephole, Ethan stood, his head bowed, hands in his pockets. Chloe opened the door and ushered him in.

He looked her up and down, as if searching for wounds. "You okay? I came as quick as I could."

She fidgeted her fingers, then stilled them and clasped her hands behind her back. This would be a hard conversation, for both of them, but it had to be done. "Yeah, everything's okay, but I was hoping we could talk?"

He frowned, but nodded and she led him to her couch.

Sinking down into the cushions, she motioned for him to do the same. He did, holding his body stiffly.

He surprised her by speaking first. "I've been worried about you." She opened her mouth to talk but he wasn't done. "And I think part of it is my fault, but I'm unsure how to fix it."

She laid a hand on his arm. "Ethan, it's not your fault. It's mine. I haven't been doing a very good at dealing with all of this."

He squinted at her. "I'm not sure it's possible to do a good job at dealing with the death of your sister."

She winced. "Right, I agree with that. But the way I've

been dealing with it has not been good." She took a deep breath. "I kept thinking about how it should have been me in that car."

He blinked at her. "What do you mean? Samantha wanted the ride and—"

"That's not what I mean."

"Then what do you mean?"

She twisted her fingers in her lap. "Of all of us, Samantha should be here. She was such a light in our family, in the world. I was always the one that blended into the background. Samantha would have made an impact on the world and—"

Ethan leaned forward "What are you talking about?"

She inhaled sharply. "Samantha would have been able to deal with this better. She was a doer, you know? So she would have done something after I died, working on holding everyone together. While all I did was retreat and try to stay in the shadows while the storm raged. And then when it was over, all the pieces of our family were scattered."

He gripped her wrist and tugged her to him. "I had no idea you thought that. What's happening between me and Mom and Dad has nothing to do with you. Well, it does because you're family, but you couldn't have prevented it. Samantha couldn't have prevented it." His voice dipped. "That's my cross to bear, not yours."

"I don't want you to have to bear it alone, though."

"Well, I hate that you thought you had to take it all." He gripped her shoulders and pulled back to look her in the eye. "Why didn't you talk to me about this?"

"I didn't want to make you feel more guilty than I know you already do, Ethan. I love you, and the last thing I wanted to do was add another burden. I didn't want you to have to worry about me." She pursed her lips. "Which I didn't really succeed in since you were worried anyway."

He smiled a little at that. "I was worried. But this… makes sense. And I'm so glad you talked to me."

"I feel better, too. I thought keeping it to myself was the right decision because of the circumstances, but now I see that I was wrong." For the first time in a long time, Chloe felt like she could breathe. Her lungs filled without that tight band that prevented her from ever taking a deep breath.

She stood up and held out her hand. "I have something else to tell you. But first, I have some chicken salad I made. Would you like a sandwich?"

He took her hand and nodded. "Sure."

In the kitchen, she grabbed a bag of rolls and the bowl of chicken salad out of the refrigerator. As she made the sandwiches, her hands were shaking. But she knew that she better tell Ethan now before he found out another way.

A chair scraped behind her, and she knew Ethan had sat at the table.

"So," she said, head bent to her task, "I've been seeing Grant."

Silence.

She'd expected a gasp. Or a curse. Or maybe a fist pound. But all she heard behind her was silence. She kept talking. "I met him at the Philly Comic-Con. I didn't know who he was then, and he didn't know who I was. But we… Well, we had a really good time together. So when we saw each other at the restaurant for dinner, it was a surprise to both of us. I think we both tried to stay away. But we haven't been great about staying away. Not at all, really. Plus, I met his daughter at that career-fair thing you made me go to. She's delightful. And likes me, which has only made this whole thing more complicated." She took a plate in each hand and turned around.

Ethan was staring out the window of her back door. His face was expressionless, a mask, when only moments ago he'd smiled.

"Ethan?" She placed his plate on the table and sat beside him. "Are you mad?"

"He didn't tell me." His voice was monotone.

"Of course he didn't tell you, Ethan. You threatened him. And I didn't want you to know either. Telling you would have been betraying me as well. And, well, Grant chose me, apparently."

"And he didn't want your number to ask you security questions."

She cleared her throat. "Uh, no. We'd had a little bit of a disagreement."

Finally, Ethan turned to her, his pale eyes piercing. "Does he treat you well?"

She picked at her sandwich. "He treats me very well." When she looked up, Ethan's eyes were closed, his hands fisted on the table. "Are you okay?"

He met her gaze. "You're a grown woman, and I can't tell you what to do. I wish you hadn't had to sneak around. That wasn't what I wanted for you."

She laid her hand on top of his fist. He relaxed it and opened his fingers, palm up. She clasped it. "We didn't sneak around because of you, not really. I haven't been ready to commit."

"And how's Grant handling all of that?"

She smiled. "He's the one who pushed me into opening up about this. I pushed him away but I'm hoping when I get my head sorted out, I'll be able to get him back."

Ethan nodded, squeezing her hand, then let it go to eat his sandwich. She did the same.

"Sydney is a firecracker, isn't she?" Ethan asked.

"Yes, she's wonderful. Was Grant married to her mother or…?"

Ethan shook his head. "One-night stand from college. The woman was going to give her up for adoption, but Grant said he'd care for the child. Sometimes I'm sure he wants to smack himself for that decision, but he's never regretted it."

"She adores him."

"As she should."

When lunch was over, Chloe cleaned up. She caught Ethan staring at the picture on the refrigerator, the one of Samantha, him, and Chloe. She knew it had taken a lot out of him to talk about their sister today. He rarely did, and she didn't push. Although she was starting to think maybe she should, because Ethan wasn't doing any better at his grief than she was.

"I'm going to visit Mom and Dad," she announced. "Leaving later today."

He was staring out the back door again, hands in his pockets. He didn't respond.

"Would you like to come?" she asked.

Even though she knew his answer, she held out hope until he shook his head.

"Maybe you could call them?" she suggested softly.

He turned to her then, eyes filled with sorrow before he threw down the shutters. "Drive safe, Chloe. Are you staying with them or at a hotel?"

It was hard for her to stay in that house, the one she'd grown up in with two other siblings. "At the house, I think."

He nodded and walked toward the door. "Please let me know when you get back into town."

She followed him. "Are you going to say anything to Grant?"

He paused with his hand on the doorknob, then turned around. "No, I don't believe I will."

"It was hard for him, I know. He didn't like not telling you. But it was my decision as much as his."

Ethan smiled slightly. "I understand. We'll see if Grant comes to me. Something tells me he will."

Chloe doubted it. She'd left Grant standing in a parking lot. If he never talked to her again, she wouldn't be surprised. But at least he'd given her the push she needed to change something about her life, even if he wasn't there for her on the other side.

Chapter Twelve

Grant admitted this was a little over the line. Dipping into obsessive territory. He wasn't driven by a lustful desire to claim Chloe or anything crazy like that.

He cared. He was worried. And he missed her.

He couldn't stop thinking about finally getting the chance to be with her—*really* be with her. The glimpse of her heart he'd gotten during her interaction with Sydney and with him at the coffee shop wasn't enough. He wanted more. He wasn't willing to give up.

And that's why he stood outside Ethan's door, biting his lip raw and holding two foil-wrapped burritos in one hand. He knocked and heard a deep voice from inside answer. "Come in!"

He opened the door and shut it behind him. A vision of Chloe dancing around in Ethan's kitchen flashed through his mind and he shook his head quickly.

Ethan was in the living room, reading a book. He laid the

worn paperback on the table beside him and leaned back in his recliner. Grant lifted a burrito toward Ethan, who shook his head. Grant shrugged and took a seat on the couch.

"Sydney says hi," Grant said.

"Yeah? Why didn't you bring her over?"

Grant took a bite and swallowed before talking. "I, uh, wanted to talk to you about something."

Ethan's expression showed nothing. "About *Gamers*?"

Shit, why was this so hard? He'd been tempted to take a dick pic before he came, just in case that was the last time he'd ever have his genitals intact. "Uh, no, it's personal."

Again, no movement on Ethan's face. The cold bastard.

Grant took a deep breath and set the burritos aside. He wasn't as hungry as he'd thought. "So I've been seeing a woman."

Not even a blink.

Grant soldiered on. "At the beginning it was kind of all physical. But then it wasn't. I really care about her, and I think I'm falling of her."

Ethan fingers tapped the armrest of the recliner.

"The problem is she's…working through some stuff. It's been a couple of days since I heard from her and I'm nervous, you know? I don't want to crowd her but I want her to know how much she means to me. How much I want this to work. And I want a way to show her that."

"And you want my opinion on how to do that?" Ethan asked.

Grant nodded.

"And you're asking me, why? I think it's pretty obvious my skills with dating are rusty. Why aren't you talking to Austin about this?"

So, it was now or never. He was really going to do this, and hopefully come out of it unscathed or at least unscarred. Maybe he should have greased up his face first, like fighters do, so Ethan didn't cut open his eyebrow with his fist.

"Well, I'm not talking to Austin about this because the woman I care about isn't *his* sister." Grant sucked in a breath. And held it. He didn't dare look away from Ethan, from those pale eyes. He'd be a man and take his hit, literally or figuratively.

But the creepy thing was that Ethan hadn't moved. He hadn't made any outward reaction to the fact that Grant had been carrying on a relationship with his precious sister behind his back.

If anything, he looked…bored.

Grant waved a hand. "Earth to Ethan? Are you there? Because… I guess I expected you to yell or something."

"Why'd you expect that?" Ethan said softly.

Grant threw up his hands. "Seriously? I'm sleeping with your sister, Ethan! I've been doing it for about a month. Granted, I had no idea she was your sister the first time it happened. We were dressed up at the Comic-Con and she was Sari and I was Breck." And oh God, he was rambling but he couldn't stop. "We tried to stay away, but neither of us wanted to. Then she tried to cut it off because she thought I wouldn't like her once I really got to know her. Which is so dumb, right? I mean, she's pretty fucking awesome and smart and sweet. I tried to get through to her a little but she shoved me away. And I'm not willing to give up."

He ran out of breath. And steam. He slumped down into the couch cushions and let his head drift back so that he stared at the ceiling.

There was nothing but silence between them until Grant said, "I'm sorry, Ethan. I'm sorry it happened and I didn't tell you. I'm sorry. But I'm not sorry for falling for your sister. Because she's everything I didn't know I wanted."

More silence, until this time, it was Ethan's voice that broke it. "She's at our parents' house."

Grant raised his head. "What?"

Ethan was fingering the dog-eared edges of his paperback, eyes on the cover. "She came over here and told me about you two."

Grant stared. Chloe had told her brother? It must have killed her to tell Ethan. Despite that, hope flared in Grant's chest.

"And then she talked to me about some other things," Ethan said. "About what she's been going through. I hadn't realized... I hadn't realized she was placing so much on her shoulders. It broke my heart, but it needed to be done." He lifted his gaze to Grant's, who stared at him dumbfounded. "She said you had something to do with that?"

"Well, I don't know about that. She confided in me a little and I told her she needed to talk to you, that you wouldn't have wanted her to be carrying around this burden."

"She said she thought it should have been her. I had no idea she felt like that."

Chloe might have been better for the conversation, but Ethan looked wrecked, and Grant didn't know how to fix that for his friend. "It was all an accident, E—"

"I don't need you to psychoanalyze me." Ethan's gaze was ice. The room dropped twenty degrees. "You can do that with Chloe because it seems to help, but don't come here and patronize me and tell me it was an accident."

"Don't get all frosty with me, you asshole. I care about you *and* Chloe."

"Well worry about Chloe, because I don't fucking need it." Ethan stood up abruptly and walked into the kitchen.

Grant closed his eyes and balled his hands on his knees. He wished Ethan would go to therapy or do something to help him deal with what happened. Instead the guy threw himself into work and generally avoided all human interaction.

If this continued, he was going to have to stage an intervention. He followed Ethan into the kitchen, realizing that calling Ethan an asshole wasn't the way to go.

Ethan stood at the sink, staring out the back window with his arms crossed.

"I'm sorry I called you an asshole. And for other things that I'm sure I still owe you apologies for," Grant said.

Ethan's lips twitched. "I'm sorry for yelling at you. You didn't deserve that."

An apology from Ethan was not unheard of but still kinda rare. Grant took the olive branch. "It's no problem, I was prodding."

Ethan sighed and opened a kitchen drawer. He rummaged around for a couple of seconds and then pulled out a pad of paper. He scribbled on it and then handed it to Grant. "This is where my parents live."

Grant frowned at it. "Why are you giving this to me?"

Ethan raised his eyebrows. "So you can go after Chloe."

"Y-you think she wants me there?"

Ethan leaned on the counter. "It's got to be hard for her there. And I'm sure she's doing her very best to handle it. But there's nothing wrong with showing up and telling her that you're there for her. Sometimes my parents…aren't so good with words. They think they're saying the right thing but it's really the exact wrong thing." Ethan stared at his hand, braced on the counter. "I think maybe we all want to know that the person we care about cares just as much."

Grant flicked the paper in his fingers. It was a three-hour drive, and he'd have to get a hotel room nearby. He didn't want to assume he could stay at the Talley's. "Can you watch Sydney overnight?"

"I'll come over and sleep on your couch. Movie night or something."

"Sydney would like that."

"Great, now go pack and rescue my sister."

Grant grinned.

Sydney's eyes were huge.

Grant rarely talked about his dating life with his daughter, because he kept it separate from her. He hadn't introduced a woman to her in years, and they both seemed okay with the arrangement.

But there was too much to this situation with Chloe. She was Ethan's sister, and no matter what happened, Grant couldn't deny that he cared about Chloe and always would, in one way or another.

So he'd come clean and told Sydney that he'd dated Chloe a few times. Sydney's response was accurate. "Oh my God, Dad, does Ethan know? He'll kill you!" Her voice was edging higher, her hands on either side of her cheeks like McCauley Caulkin in *Home Alone*.

He laughed as he pulled his duffel bag out of the back of his closet. "Yeah, he knows."

She stared at it as he tossed it on the bed. "Where are you going?"

"Ethan's coming over to watch you tonight," he said, as he pulled a couple of T-shirts out of his drawer. "I'm heading out to try to convince Chloe that I'm a model boyfriend."

Sydney's less-than-hopeful expression was not comforting.

"What's that look for? I can be very persuasive."

His daughter bit her lip. "I don't know. I get the impression Miss Talley can see through all your tricks."

"I resent that you're calling my charm *tricks*."

Sydney flopped onto the bed. "I'm excited to hang out with Ethan. Movie night?"

"He mentioned that."

"He's less grumpy when it's just him and me."

Grant paused, and then he resumed packing. He'd noticed the way Ethan warmed up around his daughter, too. Did she remind him of Samantha? "He likes you a lot, Sydney."

She popped up quickly. "Do I have time to make cookies for you to take to Chloe? Where are you going anyway?"

"I'm going to visit her at her parents', and I'd love to take some of your cookies."

Sydney clapped her hands together and ran out of the room. "I'll bake fast!" she yelled over her shoulder.

Grant chuckled and continued to pack. Every once in a while, a wave of indecision would wash over him. Was he making the right choice to go after Chloe? Maybe Ethan was sending him to his doom on purpose? But no, that was mean and while Ethan was a reclusive bastard, he wasn't a spiteful jerk.

And Grant liked the idea of reaching out to Chloe. He got that she needed to deal with her issues on her own; she'd already done an amazing job telling Ethan how she felt. But Grant didn't want her to think she had to do this all herself. Moving forward, if they were a couple…well wasn't that what a relationship was about?

Grant hadn't had a real partnership in years…or maybe he never had one? His feelings for Sydney's mother were purely platonic after that one drunken evening together. And now they only talked when it was necessary for Sydney.

He wanted that with Chloe, though. He wanted to help her with her life and get the same back in return. Sure it was selfish, but he wanted a part of her heart for himself. And in order to do that, he needed to show her how much of his she already had.

After he packed his toiletries into his bag, he zipped it up and headed downstairs. Sydney was at the counter smoothing batter into a pan. She looked up as he walked in. "Hey!"

He stood next to her and peered into the pan. "Hey yourself. What're you making?"

"Well I already had butter softening on the counter, so I whipped up a quick pan of chocolate-chip-cookie bars. How does that sound?"

Oh shit, he loved these things. It'd be a miracle if he didn't eat the whole pan on the way there.

As if sensing his thoughts, Sydney scowled. "Don't you dare eat all these in the car."

He laughed. "You know me so well."

She huffed and handed him the spatula to lick, which he happily did as she placed the pan into the preheated oven.

She set the timer and announced, "You can leave in fifty minutes."

What the hell was he going to do for fifty minutes? But Sydney was so pleased with herself, cheeks flushed, that he resigned himself to wait around until the damn things were done.

He helped her clean up and as she was loading the dishwasher, she tossed her braid over her shoulder and looked at him. "She emailed me, you know."

"Who?"

"Miss Talley!"

"Oh, right. Emailed you about what?"

"The recipe for the chicken fajitas."

Grant's mouth watered. "Please, please make them."

Sydney smirked. "If you convince Miss Talley to call you her boyfriend, then I'll make you chicken fajitas."

He gasped in mock outrage. "Bribery."

She giggled. "I think that's excellent incentive."

He wasn't going to tell Sydney the best incentive, which was sex with Chloe. Although, admittedly, fajitas were like sex in his mouth.

They spent the next forty-five minutes or so playing *Aric's Revenge*. Grant loved to watch Sydney play, her tongue poked out the corner of her mouth as her brow furrowed in concentration. She'd forget to blink, so then she'd have to rub her eyes and blink them rapidly to get the moisture back.

The oven timer beeped at the same time a knock came at the door.

"I'll get the cookie bars!" Sydney announced, running in to the kitchen.

Grant let in Ethan, who spotted Grant's bag inside the front door. He didn't say anything, but he did smile.

Grant hadn't worked this hard for a woman's family approval in…well, ever.

When they walked in to the kitchen, Sydney was staring at the pan. "I was going to cut them into squares and put them that cute tin I have, but they aren't cool enough for that."

Grant and Ethan just stared at her.

She rolled her eyes. "Well, at least I used my nice maroon stoneware." She pulled out the tinfoil and rolled out a piece, laying it on top and crimping the edge. "Okay, so you'll just have to let it cool on the way and then you can cut it there. Make sure you use a sharp knife and—"

"I planned to just stick my face in the pan and gnaw on it," Grant said.

Sydney glared.

He bent down and kissed her cheek. "Be good, kid. Be nice to Ethan."

"I will; have fun and drive safe."

She was such a mother hen already. He tugged her braid and then turned to Ethan. "Take care of my girl."

Ethan gazed at him steadily. "Will do. Take care of mine."

Chapter Thirteen

The only sound in the kitchen was the scraping of utensils on plates. When the clock on the wall chimed, Chloe startled, the sound cutting through the deafening silence.

She'd arrived at her parents the previous night, slept in the next day, and now it was lunch.

A silent, awkward lunch.

It'd been too long since she visited. Everything she wanted to talk about involved Ethan but the sound of his name made her parents bristle. Which in turn made her feel guilty.

She stuck a forkful of macaroni and cheese in her mouth and chewed, even though she could barely taste it. She'd been so motivated by her conversation with Grant that it had been easier to talk to Ethan than she expected. But now, facing her parents, she was grasping at her waning strength, barely remembering the reason she'd come.

Maybe she wasn't ready to let go, to give up on fixing

her family. So she extended her heart again, hoping her parents didn't crush it. "Would you want to come visit me?" she asked. "We could go out to dinner…with Ethan."

Her mother looked at her with the same pale blue eyes she'd given to her son. "I'm not sure that's the best idea."

Chloe tried to sound firm, but instead her voice rose in a whine, wobbling on each word. "He's suffering, Mom. I know he is and maybe if—"

"And we're not suffering?" her mom asked.

Chloe looked at her mother. Really looked her. Celeste Talley had always been a beautiful woman. Maybe a little regal. And now her hair was streaked with gray. Her face lined, the skin of her neck wrinkled and loose. Her hands—it was always the hands that showed age first—were lined with veins.

Her father, Martin Talley, was the same—wrinkled face, bifocals resting on the tip of his nose as he eyed Chloe from across the table. He walked stiffer now, his back bothering him.

They were good parents, if not a little strict. But they were still their own people. They weren't perfect and they held grudges. And sometimes those grudges were against their own children.

She wanted to yell at them, to tell them they weren't following the script. That they should be gathering their remaining children close and cherishing them. That they were slowly killing Ethan. She hadn't done any of that. She hadn't told them the truth. She'd tried to shove Ethan at them, force-feed them a new relationship. And that wasn't working at all. All she was doing was breaking her own heart in the process.

She dropped her fork onto her plate and willed the tears to stay at bay. She couldn't think of a single thing to say to her parents in that moment.

The doorbell rang.

Her father frowned and stood up. "I'll get it."

Chloe watched her mother, who took a sip of her water, then touched her hair as if to compose herself.

There was the sound of the front door. A murmur of male voices. Then her father poked his head into the kitchen. "Visitor here. For Chloe."

Chloe frowned. No one knew she was here. No one but Ethan...

"Who is it?" she asked, wiping her mouth and standing up.

"One of Ethan's friends. But he says he's here to see you."

Chloe tripped on the chair leg and had to grab the table to steady herself. Ethan had about two friends. Grant and Austin. And she doubted Austin was here to see her...

When she walked into the living room, Grant was standing with his back to her, peering at the pictures on the fireplace mantel. She stopped abruptly and stared.

She felt like a teenager whose prom date had just shown up.

Except she was wearing a pair of cutoff jean shorts and an oversize T-shirt, he was wearing a pair of cargo shorts, and they'd previously had dirty sex in a nightclub supply closet.

Okay, so maybe it wasn't like the prom-date thing at all.

She stood there frozen as Grant turned around to face her.

Her parents were in the kitchen behind her, talking

quietly, which was nice because it gave her a chance to greet Grant without an audience.

It'd only been a couple of days since she'd seen him, but yet seeing his face made her want to leap into his arms. And it kind of hit her like a brick wall how much she wanted to do that as Chloe. Not in any sort of role, but as herself. She wanted to leap to see if he'd catch her.

It'd been Grant who'd called her beautiful and Grant that made her come so hard she saw stars. And it was Grant who'd asked her for more. For a chance to try.

It'd been a long time since she trusted her own instincts, before she allowed herself to do what was in her heart and not worry about everyone else. A minute ago, she'd wanted to cry. But just the sight of Grant was enough to flip her emotions to the other extreme. She didn't know why he was here, but it didn't matter because he *was*.

And in that moment, her instinct was to grab Grant's hand and kiss him hard. *Really* hard. And maybe nibble on that chin and chap her lips on his scruff. Yeah, that sounded good.

She took off at a run in her bare feet. Grant's eyes widened, but he must've known what was coming, because he braced himself with a foot behind him, his hands out, as she took a jump and slammed into him.

He caught her.

His arms wrapped around her, and she hooked her ankles around his waist.

And then she was kissing him. She, Chloe Talley, was kissing the Ken-like Grant Osprey and it was everything she hadn't imagined she'd ever have.

Because Grant was kissing back, chuckling into her

mouth, the vibration tickling her tongue until she was laughing herself.

He pulled back, his eyes sparkling. "Goddamn, it's good to hear you laugh."

She pressed her lips together, her shoulders still shaking.

He raised his eyebrows. "And honestly, I think this should be a new rule."

"What should?"

"Every time you see me, I expect a running leap."

"I did a pretty good job, didn't I? Like a gazelle."

He threw back his head and boomed a laugh at the ceiling. "Exactly like a gazelle, sweetheart."

As he helped her down, he stepped back and surveyed her outfit. She stared at her bare feet, toenails painted a pale pink.

"Damn you look sweet, Chloe." His voice was a whisper, and she lifted her gaze to his.

"You look pretty sweet yourself." She brushed his hand with hers. "How did you know I was here?"

He scratched the back of his head, his mouth quirking into a nervous grin. "I, uh, went to Ethan."

"Y-you what?"

"Hey, don't act so surprised. You beat me to the punch line by telling him about us."

"Wh—"

"I went there, freaking out. Did this whole big-speech thing and then found out you'd already told him about us. You could have given me a heads-up," he groused.

He was pouting, just a little bit, and she found it adorable. "I'm sorry. I…had a lot to talk to him about."

He grabbed her hand. "It's okay. I'm glad you told him.

Because then I knew where to find you. Thought you'd throw me out, so the leap thing was welcome."

"Why'd you come?"

"Because…" He squeezed her hand. "I can't imagine how hard this is for you. Ethan not speaking to your parents. Being here, where you grew up. And…Samantha." He blew out a breath. "I wanted you to know that I'm thinking of you. And you're not alone. And if there's anything I can do, I'm all yours."

I'm all yours. His warm hand grasping hers, his voice, his smile, everything reminded her of why she was here.

"But why?" she asked. "Why do you want to be there for me? I'm a mess."

He squeezed her hand. "Because I care about you." He kissed her forehead. "Because I think you have the biggest heart of anyone I've ever met." He kissed each eyelid, then the tip of her nose. "And I tried so fucking hard not to, but I think I'm falling in love with you, Chloe."

She sucked in a breath at his words, reeling from what they all meant. When she spoke, her voice shook. "You're falling in love with Sari and Sara. Not Chloe."

He sighed, and his lips twisted into a small smile. "They're all a part of you. I'm not separating them. Chloe, I don't give a fuck what roles you played with me. That was your body and your mind and that was all you, the same woman who loves her family so much she's placed all their problems on her shoulders. The woman who does penetrative testing."

Chloe pressed her lips together to suppress a smile. He must have caught it because he grinned and kept talking. "The woman who drives me out of my mind. They are all you. And I'm falling in love with every piece of you."

Never in her life did Chloe think that was a speech she'd hear. Not by a man as good as Grant, as amazing as Grant. Her whole body felt hot and electric, like a live wire. And really, the only way to celebrate was to…well, kiss him.

As Chloe.

So she grabbed the back of his head and didn't let go. She parted her lips and the kiss deepened. And then she… lost it. Because this was her, Chloe, pouring her heart into his mouth, down his throat. He clutched her to his chest and held her face in the palm of his hot hand. And he returned the kiss as passionately as she was giving it.

And fuck, if this was how they kissed as Grant and Chloe, she couldn't wrap her brain around how they'd make love as Grant and Chloe. She wanted to get naked now, and might have if she wasn't standing in her parents' living room.

She broke the kiss and Grant panted against her lips. "Tell me this isn't just me. Tell me you're falling for me, too, Chloe."

When she licked her lips, her tongue touched his. "It's not just you, Grant. It's not just you."

His fingers flexed against the skin of her cheek "You working on reclaiming your heart for yourself? Because it's yours, Chloe. It's yours and not anyone else's."

"You still want some of my heart if I give it to you?" she asked.

"I'll just borrow," he said softly. "And I'll take good care of it."

"There's one thing yet I have to do," she said, slowly separating her body from his. "I'm sorry because I don't know if it's fair to ask you to wait—"

"I've waited thirty-two years for you. I can wait a little

longer, okay?"

He was better than Ken, way better. "Okay."

He gestured toward a foil-covered dish on the coffee table. "Those are from Sydney. She made chocolate-chip-cookie bars. I'll, uh, leave them here."

"You don't have to leave, I—"

"I'll say hi to your parents, and then I'll leave. It's okay. There are some things I can do in town before I head back tomorrow. I'm staying over at the Comfort Inn off Monroe Street. I just wanted to see you." His lips quirked. "Touch you."

"I liked seeing you and touching you."

He smiled and pressed his forehead to hers.

Her parents wandered in from the kitchen then, and she introduced Grant as "the man she'd been dating." Which sounded lame and was slightly inaccurate, but she didn't have a better explanation, or one she could say in front of her parents.

But now Chloe thought maybe…they *had* been dating, just in a very unconventional way. Despite their roles, she felt like she knew Grant enough to want to know him better. And she figured that was half the battle with dating anyway.

Then tension in the room lingered, especially when Grant mentioned he owned a business with Ethan.

Months ago, even weeks ago, Chloe would have been embarrassed at her parents' reaction to Ethan's name. She would have tried to smooth it over while her heart cracked under the strain.

But Grant was there, his hand in hers, his presence reminding her that it was time to give up the responsibility she'd unnecessarily taken on herself. It wasn't about her, what happened between Ethan and her parents.

When she walked Grant to the front door, he kissed her, a chaste one on her lips. "I'll wait for you," he said quietly. And she nodded, barely restraining herself from running after him as he walked out the door.

But she needed more time. And she wasn't finished with her parents yet.

After Grant left, Chloe wandered into the backyard of her parents' house to look for her parents. They lived on an acre of property. When she was little, her mother's backyard garden had been small, mostly located along the back of the house, so that the kids could play in the rest of it without messing up Mom's flowers.

Once all three children left the nest, her mom had reclaimed the backyard. The *entire* backyard. There were a couple of stone paths and some trees with patches of grass surrounding the base but the rest of the backyard was full of flower beds. Some were full of wildflowers, free and without too much fussing, while other beds were carefully laid out and tended to.

Chloe ran her hand over a tall bunch of zebra grass, the blades tickling her palm.

"So you're happy in Willow Park?" her mom asked, perched on a stone bench along the edge of the walk.

"Yes, I like it. There's a great market where I can get fresh produce grown locally. I might sign up for a CSA next year." She was kind of babbling. "And I like being near Ethan."

Her mother turned away.

Chloe took a deep breath, remembering Grant's hand in hers. She needed to take back her life, her heart. And she had to be honest. "Mom, you're losing Ethan, you know."

Her mother didn't move, not even a twitch, as she gazed away from Chloe, looking over her garden.

"You and Dad know that, right? You lost a daughter, and by continuing this…silent treatment, you're losing your son, too."

A muscle twitched in her mother's neck. It was something.

Chloe stepped forward and sat on the bench beside her mother. "I'm sorry for that. I'm so sorry this all happened, but it did. Samantha's gone." Her mother's body shuddered and Chloe placed her hand over her mother's where it rested on her thigh. "I can't do this anymore, though, this running around, mending holes in this family, because no matter how hard I try, I'm not the one who can fix it."

Her mother finally turned her head. Pale eyes watery. "I know you've been trying, Chloe."

"You do?" Resentment bubbled up, but she forced it down. "And you let me scramble and stress and worry?"

Her mother shook her head, blinking rapidly now. "I thought that's what you wanted, that it gave you a purpose — "

"Sure it gave me a purpose, but it was also slowly chipping away at me. And it took a hell of a lot for me to realize that if I didn't stop taking on this responsibility, that'd it would kill me."

Her mother turned then, her eyes wide I alarm. "I had no idea it was like that for you."

"Well now you know. And unless you want to lose me, too, I'm done. I'm done trying to fix you and Dad and Ethan. I can't control that. I can control me, though, and I'm taking back that control so I can finally be happy."

"I want you to be happy, I…" Her mother seemed at a loss for words.

"This is why I avoided saying all this to you, and to Ethan. Because the last thing I wanted to do was add more guilt and more sadness and more emotion, but I can't do it anymore, Mom."

Her mother embraced her. "I'm sorry."

Chloe closed her eyes and hugged back. "I am, too." She pulled back. "So you and Ethan…I'm stepping away from it. I love you and Dad. I love Ethan. I can love you separately."

Her mother's lip shifted. "It's complicated. I…don't know what we're able to do. The pain is too much still."

Chloe knew all about pain. "I know, Mom. I know." Her parents weren't going to repair their relationship with Ethan for her. They had to do it because they wanted to. So Chloe was done trying to mend holes with thin threads that broke every time she tied them.

When she left her parents' house that evening, she was still in mourning, but at least she was doing something. Chloe mourned her sister, she mourned the death of the family she once had. Samantha's death had ripple effects Chloe wasn't sure anyone was prepared for. And now Chloe realized she had to let go. Release her fingers where she'd been white-knuckling her hold on the family she had before, the family she'd never get back. And she had to fall.

She hoped she landed on her feet. And she hoped Grant was there at the bottom like he said he'd be.

Time to find out.

Chapter Fourteen

Grant leaned back against the pillows on the hotel bed that night and flicked through the channels. The remote wasn't working well; the batteries were probably dying. He smacked it a couple of times on his palm. He stretched his arm over his head and crossed his legs. He'd changed into a pair of sweatpants and nothing else, determined to lay on this bed and do absolutely nothing until he fell asleep.

There wasn't much on TV—movies he'd seen a dozen times, a baseball game he didn't care about. If he hadn't just hung up the phone with Sydney, he'd call her again. Except that was pretty lame. She was in the middle of movie night with Ethan, so she didn't need her bored dad cramping her style.

He knew now that it was the right decision to go after Chloe today. The look on her face when she'd seen him… He wished he'd had a camera. And now, he'd give her time. She hadn't pushed him away, she'd given him hope. So he'd head home tomorrow, and hopefully Chloe would show up. Hopefully.

There was a knock on his hotel room door. He frowned and then climbed off the bed to pad toward the door. He didn't remember ordering anything. He had plenty of towels.

He opened the door a crack and peered out into the hallway.

His heart soared quickly and then plummeted just as fast.

Sari stood in the hallway. She wore the same lace-up boots. That same skirt with the slit up the thigh. That same corset that made her breasts look fantastic. Her hair was long—fake this time—and her eyes were rimmed with a thick layer of eyeliner.

Except…he didn't want Sari.

He wanted Chloe.

"Can I come in?" she asked.

His heart hurt. She didn't get it. She still wanted games, but he was tired of them. After all they'd said to each other, after he'd chased her three hours to her parents' house, she still showed up at his hotel dressed like someone else.

He thought about closing the door in her face. He almost did. But instead he hung his head and stepped back, letting her pass.

When she walked by him into the room, he smelled strawberries. And that hurt even more.

He closed the door behind her and rested his hand against it, head bowed. This wasn't what he wanted, not at all.

There was a thump and he looked up. She dropped a leather bag on the bed and looked at him, twisting her hands nervously. "Hello."

"Hi," his voice cracked. "Look, I—"

"So I'm Sari," she said.

He swallowed, clenching his fists at his sides. He wanted to yell, to kick her out. But there was something in her voice…something he couldn't place, which made him do nothing but nod.

"This is Sari," she said again, gesturing to her clothes.

He nodded again.

And that's when she reached up and took her wig off.

He couldn't breathe; he couldn't do anything but stand there as that black mop of hair fell to the floor at her feet. Then she took off her boots, slowly, unlacing them until they lay slumped under the desk and she stood in bare feet. The corset came off next, which she did herself this time, reaching behind her back, her brow furrowed as she unlaced it. That went on the desk carefully.

She was topless now, those breasts he loved on full display. But he wasn't fully hard, not at all. Because this…this wasn't sexual, he realized. She was doing something, making some sort of statement so he said nothing as she slipped off the skirt and stood before him in nothing but a small pair of panties.

She bent and unzipped the bag at the end of the bed. Her hands were shaking, the zipper clicking as she wet a cotton ball with some sort of liquid and rubbed it over her face. The makeup, the heavy black on her eyes, the red lips, the rouged cheeks. It all came off on a couple of cotton balls, which she tossed into the small trash can beside the desk.

She swallowed, staring at him, her eyes red and shining. Her lips trembled and he wanted to reach out to her but her body language was telling him to stay back, so he did.

She took a deep breath, pulled out a pair of loose cotton pants, slid them on, and then tugged a large black T-shirt over her head that said in white lettering, *There's no place like 127.0.0.1.*

Her shoulders shook now, her eyes brimming over with tears. Her lips formed an *O*, as she took a couple of breaths to settle herself. And then she looked him right in the eye and said, "Hi, Grant Osprey. I'm Chloe Talley. Nice to meet you."

. . .

She was fully clothed. In fact, this was one of the few times she'd been fully clothed in front of Grant. And yet, she'd never felt so naked. Not ever.

There was no costume. No persona. No attitude. This was Chloe. As Grant should have met her the first time.

Her hands shook, and she couldn't stop worrying the in- side of her cheek but despite all of that, she knew she was in the right place.

Her nerves meant she realized how important this was.

Grant hadn't moved yet. He stared at her, that blue stare the most intense she'd ever seen. His usual humor was non- existent on his face. This was serious. This meant something.

Last time they were in a hotel room, she'd walked toward him, while he stood taking her with undisguised lust. That was all it had been then.

Now, there was a whole lot more to the look in Grant's eyes.

This time, when she took a step forward, he took one, too, and they both kept walking until they met in the middle at the foot of the king-size bed.

Grant was smiling down at her while he cupped her cheek and she hadn't realized it was possible for someone to look at her like that. The way he drank her in, soaked her up, well, she wasn't sure how she'd lived without all this time.

She reached up and gripped his wrist with her fingers, leaning into his hand.

"Hi, Chloe," he said. "I've never seen anyone more beautiful than you right now."

She tried to stop the tears, but they came anyway. She'd known this would be hard, but she hadn't expected to be this emotional. She hadn't expected to feel so raw and exposed but she should have known. This was Grant after all. He'd always been able to see right through every facade she threw up.

"I'm sorry it took me so long," she said. "But I had to put my heart back together. I had to get my head straight, before I could commit to you. And I'm still nervous. I'm still worried that I'm not going to be everything you need. But I want to try."

Grant shook his head, the tender expression never leaving his face. "I don't need anything. I just want. I want you, Chloe. All of you."

She didn't even flinch when he said her name while his thumb caressed the corner of her mouth. It felt...good. And right. Her heart was definitely back in her chest, because now it was beating double-time at his words. It was her — Chloe — present in that moment with Grant. How had she gotten so lucky?

He wore only a pair of sweats slung low on his hips. She ran her hands up his stomach, over his chest, before laying her palms on his shoulders.

"When you took off your shirt in the hotel room that first time, I got into the role and imagined you had these muscles from, you know, Aric's grand revenge plot." She brushed his biceps with the backs of her hands. "I pretended these were from wielding your mighty sword." She trailed her fingers down his torso and then patted his thighs. "That these legs were from riding your trusty steed."

"Midnight," he said softly.

"Yes, your horse Midnight." She smiled. "And now, well I think these arms are from helping Sydney stir a particularly tough batter and these legs are from climbing your stairs or pacing your office."

"Chloe…" he whispered, his voice full of reverence.

"I like the reality better than the fiction," she said. "And I'm not sure I ever thought I'd say that."

"Fuck, I need to kiss you," he growled and then his hands were fisting her hair and his lips were on hers, his tongue pressing into his mouth. Her skin was tight and hot all over. She wanted her clothes off. She wanted to touch him as much as possible, full contact.

She ripped herself from his kiss and tore her completely nerdy T-shirt over her head. Grant got the silent memo because he shoved down his sweatpants, stepping out of them like they were fire.

His cock was hard, standing out from his belly like a proud soldier. She kicked off her pants and underwear, then grabbed his shaft, and stroked it once. He groaned and they fell to the bed in a tangle of limbs, with Grant's body on top of hers.

He gripped her shoulders, pinning her to the bed, effectively slowing the frenzy. She rocked her hips and he moaned. "Chloe, hold on. I want this to be slow, okay? Slow."

Slow sex was a new concept to her. Fast was the game, get in, get some, and get out before the clock struck midnight and the carriage turned back into pumpkin.

Except she didn't feel like a pumpkin. She was Chloe, naked with the man of her dreams and yeah…she wanted this to last, too.

"You're right," she said breathlessly.

He blew out a calming breath and then began the torture.

If anything happened to Grant, she was going to donate his tongue to science—mental note to ask him if he was an organ donor—because that thing needed to be studied.

He was wicked with it, tracing her collarbone, circling her hard nipples. He dipped it into her bellybutton as she tangled her fingers in his hair.

And then he grinned up at her before sticking his face between her legs and giving her the best oral sex of her lifetime.

He was a master at knowing how fast, how much pressure, and exactly where that little bundle of nerves was that made her toes curl. This time, he added fingers, curling them inside until he touched that same spot he had before, the one no one had ever found. And the dual stimulation had her drenched, writhing on his hand and tongue until she was whimpering in a hoarse voice.

She was so turned on, and the orgasm was such a slow build, that she wasn't even sure it had hit her until Grant said, "Yeah, that's it, I can feel it, sweetheart, come for me."

Her muscles were squeezing his fingers and sounds were coming out of her mouth that might have been prayers. She wasn't sure.

Grant crawled up her body, massaging her thighs. He was grinning, lips red. "How're you doing?"

"I'm pretty good." She sounded like a frog.

"Did you lose your voice already, Princess? Good thing you don't have to talk to do your job because man, I'm not even close to being finished with you."

She grabbed his neck and crushed his lips to hers, tasting herself and not caring.

She wrapped her legs around his hips. His hard cock rubbed along her wet, sensitive flesh. She rolled her hips and smiled against his lips when he groaned.

"Go get a condom and claim your woman."

Grant laughed and was off the bed in a shot, running into the bathroom. He came out holding a condom, grinning like an idiot. "You're lucky I keep one in my bag." He rolled it on as he knee-walked between her legs on the bed. He dropped to all fours, hands on either side of her head. "Hey there, Chloe."

She ran her hand through her hair and let it rest on the bed above her head. "Hi, Grant."

He closed his eyes slowly, then fired her with the blue laser when they popped back open. "I think that's the first time you said my name to me," he said softly.

She felt the smile drop off her face as her stomach rolled. She hadn't realized she hadn't even said his name. This man was definitely her dream man for still wanting her after all this. "Really?"

"It's okay," he said. "You're saying it now."

"Grant." She licked her lips, tasting his name on her lips, savoring it on her tongue. "Grant, Grant, Grant—"

He cut her off by kissing her and entering her at the same time.

She gasped into his mouth and clutched her shoulders. When he began to move his hips, there was no rush to the rhythm. He pulled back so he could watch her face. He'd stop when he was in to the hilt, grind his hips, then pull back out, each thrust a blow to her mind and her body.

Because the whole time, he was whispering things like, "beautiful" and "gorgeous" and "I dreamed about this" and "thank you, Chloe."

And she thought about saying, *I love you, Grant.*

But there was time. There was plenty of time, so instead she watched his face, this beautiful, caring man who wanted her.

So when he whispered, "Say my name," she didn't hesitate.

"Grant," she said through a lump in her throat.

"Fuck yes," he whispered. He shoved his face into her neck, bit her skin, and she came. She came apart on Grant's cock plunging inside of her, Grant's breath in her ear, Grant's breath saying her name like a prayer.

And then it was Grant who came inside of her on a long moan, whose hips stuttered. And it was Grant who stroked her hair as she burst into tears.

• • •

Chloe's fingers grazed Grant's chest as he lay on his back. Every once in a while, he'd feel a nail, but mostly, it was soft touches, like a feather.

He squeezed her tighter to his chest and closed his eyes.

He couldn't remember a time when the sex had been... like *that*. Sex where he stared into his partner's eyes. Sex where the journey was better than the destination. Sex where hearing his own name was like coming home.

He liked rough sex. He liked dirty talk. Chloe did, too, if their previous encounters were any indication. But to know now that they could also have sex like this, where they took their time, where they—Jesus Christ, *made love*—well then wasn't that the ultimate?

He hadn't realized he wanted that, the type of lovemaking they'd just done. But now that they had, he couldn't imagine living without it.

Chloe shifted in his arms so she could look him in the eye. "So, are we going to try this?"

He cupped her cheek. "Yeah, we are. I want to take you out to a fancy dinner. I want to snuggle with you on the couch under a blanket while we watch bad action movies. I want to see you in my kitchen, cooking with my daughter."

Her eyes were wide. "I want those things, too."

"And you're okay dating a washed-up single dad?"

She rolled her eyes. "You're not washed up, you're thirty-two. I love your daughter, and I love what a great dad you are."

"Sydney's more my parent. I think my only use to her is taste-tester."

"I highly doubt that."

"You just wait until you're there and she yells at me for leaving my boxers on the floor of the bedroom. She shames me."

Chloe's laughter was musical as it rang out in the hotel

room.

"I like making you laugh," he said.

"I like when you make me laugh," she answered.

"Yeah? Well I have this hotel room until tomorrow morning so there's plenty of time to make you laugh a lot. Hard and fast and slow. Maybe...about three times."

Chloe bit her lip. "Is this what I have to look forward to with dating a single dad? You using euphemisms for orgasm."

Grant shook his head. "Nah, Sydney's smarter than me. She'd see right through them. So, how about those three times?"

She pressed a kiss to the corner of his mouth. "I like even numbers."

He rolled his eyes. "God, fine. Just give me, like, half an hour of recovery time."

She hopped off the bed and began digging in her bag again. "Hey," he leaned up on his elbows, "maybe twenty minutes if you don't put clothes on again."

She grinned and pulled out a clear plastic tub. "I brought fuel."

"Fuel?"

She threw the tub at him and then crawled onto the bed. He pulled off the lid and breathed in the smell of choco-late chip cookies. "Oh my God, I'm getting hard again over chocolate."

Chloe winked at him and reached into the container, grabbing a cookie and taking a bite. "You brought me treats at my parents' and I figured I'd repay the favor."

"I definitely love you."

"You were unsure before?"

He shoved a cookie into his mouth so he didn't have to

answer that.

When they'd scarfed down several cookies, Chloe rested her head on his stomach. "I thought of you as a Ken doll when we first met," Chloe said, her breath hot on his chest.

He looked down at her as she propped her chin on a fist to meet his gaze. "A Ken doll?"

"Yeah, you know, all blond-haired and blue-eyed with a square jaw."

"Did you play with Barbies a lot when you were little?"

She nodded. "They always ended up naked on the rooftop of my Dream House. Because I had a Skipper, too, and what they did on the rooftop wasn't appropriate for her little eyes."

His little sex fiend. "Ken's kind of a hard ideal to live up to, isn't he?"

Chloe scrunched her nose. "Not really. When I take off your pants, I'm much happier at what I see than when I took off Ken's pants."

Grant figured he should be grateful about that. "Poor Ken."

"Poor Barbie," Chloe muttered.

He laughed, hard. And Chloe laughed, her green eyes scrunched, her mouth wide.

She sobered then. "Were you serious about coming to grief counseling with me?"

"Of course I was. I'd come with you in a heartbeat."

"Thank you."

He rolled onto his side so they faced each other. "Thanks for not throwing me out of your parents' house when I showed up unannounced."

"I wouldn't have done that."

He tongued the roof of his mouth as he thought about the right way to word what he planned to say next. "You know, I don't have a problem with role-playing again. Or anything you want to do, really. That was fun, right?"

Chloe's cheeks stained pink, but she nodded.

"And this… Well damn, I've never had what we just did and I think that's why I was so stubborn about not playing the game anymore, Chloe. Because I didn't want to just play for your body, I wanted to play for your heart."

"Grant…" she whispered.

"And I feel like now I got some of it, even if it was just a little bit. And I hope I did what I told you I would. I hope I gave some of mine back."

Her eyes were wet, really wet, and she was blinking a lot. He didn't apologize though, because he wasn't sorry. Not at all.

"You did, Grant," she said, her voice still a little hard. "You did."

He kissed her nose, then her lips, then nibbled on her ear, until she began shifting her legs restlessly.

"So, even numbers, right?" he asked.

"Two down, two to go," she said.

He hummed as he settled between her legs and palmed her breasts. "Guess I got work to do then."

Epilogue

Chloe snipped off a couple of buds of the rhododendron bush and eyed the plant critically.

Grant's house, while beautiful, had been severely lacking in the landscaping department. He'd tried to say he didn't care about gardens and flowers. But when she was out there, on her hands and knees digging in the dirt, he found numerous reasons to be out there with her.

Most of those reasons involved standing behind her, commenting appreciatively on the size and shape of her ass.

As she dropped on all fours to pull a rogue weed from in front of the black-eyed Susans, Grant whistled from behind her.

"That's great, sweetheart. Now maybe arch your back a little more."

"Don't you have something better to do?" she huffed.

A pause, then. "Nope, pretty sure I have absolutely nothing better to do."

She rolled her eyes, but she smiled. Her body had never been a source of self-consciousness for her, no that had been all focused on what was inside, but Grant's approval and compliments on every part of her, inside and out, still filled her with warmth.

It'd been a year since that day he'd followed her to her parents. In that time, she'd moved in with him and Sydney. Ethan had frowned at that, saying it was too fast, but she and Grant had been through a lot together and no one made her feel as valued as Grant did.

Even if right now, her value was apparently her ass.

"Wow, there are a lot of weeds, here, huh? You're going to be on your knees for a while." Grant tsked. "Such a shame."

She wiggled her ass and he groaned. "Don't tempt me right now. We're outside and it's the middle of the day—"

She began to roll her hips and looked at him coyly over her shoulder.

His eyes were narrowed, a bead of sweat dripping down his temple. He wore a T-shirt and a pair of shorts, his hair adorably rumpled, and his eyes were on her ass.

"Later tonight," he said, his voice low, "I expect you just like this on the bed, naked, and I'll spend a good half hour with my mouth between your legs."

She never got tired of that mouth. What it did and the words it said. "You promising?" she asked.

His gaze lifted to hers. "Oh definitely."

She smiled at him, then straightened up quickly as the back door of the house slammed open. "Dad! Chloe!" Sydney's voice carried on the breeze.

"Around the side of the house!" Grant called. He

pointed at Chloe and whispered, "This isn't over."

"'Course not." She winked at him.

He scowled at her as Sydney came into view as she bounded off the deck. "Hey, the cookies have been in the fridge for an hour, so we can bake them now."

Chloe stood up, brushing the dirt from her gloves. The recipe they'd used had called for chilled dough and Sydney had been impatient. "Sure, just let me get cleaned up."

She baked with Sydney as much as she could. Sydney taught her the exacting method of baking while she taught Sydney the more creative, free-flowing method of cooking.

It was fun, their bonding time, and Grant seemed to enjoy watching them.

He followed them into the house like a puppy, surely hoping to steal a little cookie dough.

Chloe scrubbed her hands in the kitchen sink while Sydney retrieved the bowl from the refrigerator.

The diamond on Chloe's hand glittered under the water. Grant had proposed a couple of months ago.

They'd be married next year. Chloe would be an Osprey. And she couldn't wait.

She and Sydney set to work without much conversing, rolling the dough into balls and placing them on a parchment-lined cookie sheet. When Chloe first moved in, there had been an adjustment period. Sydney was used to having her father all to herself. This house was her house, if anything, and Chloe had been more like a guest than a resident for a couple of months.

Sydney liked Chloe, but it was one thing to respect her and another to have to share her father's attention with another female.

But with time, they all established a new routine.

She looked up from the pan to where Grant sat at the kitchen table, reading the newspaper. "Have you talked to Ethan lately?"

Grant frowned. "He's been avoiding me."

She sighed. "Me, too."

"I think we need to storm his castle before he turns into a beast and the natives come after him with pitchforks."

She wanted to laugh, but it wasn't funny. Ethan had been worse lately, more grouchy, more reclusive, and no matter how hard she tried to drag him out of his house, he'd been excellent at resisting.

Chloe sighed. They were meeting Austin and Marley at a bar tonight to celebrate Marley's brother's birthday. Chloe had met Chad Lake once or twice and he was always entertaining. She had tried to convince Ethan to come, too. That hadn't gone over well. He said he'd stay and watch Sydney, even thought she was old enough to stay home by herself. Chloe didn't argue.

She loved Ethan, but she could only do so much. And if she learned anything in the past year, it was that she needed to stop preventing her own happiness for the sake of others.

Because this life? Well, she'd fought for it. And it was totally worth it.

Acknowledgments

I think I have to thank the readers first. Because you all are the reason I have so much fun writing this series. You responded to Marley and Austin in CHANGING HIS GAME and you all wanted Grant and Chad and Ethan and I'm excited to say, "Yes, yes, I'm giving them to you!"

Thanks to Heather Howland for loving my nerds as much as I do. You are a master-editor and I've learned so much from you. Thanks for sticking it out with me when Chloe and Grant gave us fits.

Thank you to Marisa Corvisiero who's my best cheerleader.

Natalie Blitt, the plot whisperer, thank you for helping me figure out how to end this book. Your ideas spurned my favorite grand gesture I've ever written. Chloe and Grant thank you as well.

Thanks to all my Mobsters in Meg's Mob. I adore you all and you push me every day.

To my husband—thanks for your technology knowledge. Who knew four years of a computer science degree would lead to you feeding me technology puns for my erotic romance? Haha. I love you.

About the Author

Megan Erickson worked as a journalist covering real-life dramas before she decided she liked writing her own endings better and switched to fiction.

She lives in Pennsylvania with her husband, two kids and two cats. When she's not tapping away on her laptop, she's probably listening to the characters in her head who won't stop talking.

For more, visit www.meganerickson.org or sign up for her newsletter at eepurl.com/KNN9P

CHANGING HIS GAME

Getting caught with a dirty GIF by the smoking-hot IT guy is a whole new level of awkward for Marley Lake. What she doesn't know is that Austin Rivers is a secret partner—and technically her boss. One look at that GIF, though, and he's ready to install a lot more than just software. But with Marley's promotion and reputation on the line, Austin will have to find a way to change his game...or risk losing the only woman with the cheat code to his heart.